There was something in his voice.

Slowly, Jillie moved closer, willing him to look at her, her breath catching in her throat, her heart pounding. Had that been *regret* she'd heard?

When Seb finally met her gaze, she realized it had been a false hope. He looked no different than he always did.

Damn him. In that instant, more than anything, she wanted his expression to change.

"Seb?"

He cocked his head, waiting patiently, a perfect soldier robot—unfeeling.

That was the last straw.

Though she knew he understood intellectually how much danger she'd been in tonight, she wanted him to *feel*—even just a little bit.

So Jillie, with adrenaline still simmering in her blood, did what she'd been wanting to do ever since she'd first laid eyes on him.

She grabbed him and then kissed him. Certain and sure, willing him to react.

After a moment, he did.

Dear Reader,

Sometimes people blow into your life like a tornado. They arrive so fast, treat you to their own vibrant brand of happiness, and then disappear on the next gust of wind, leaving you to miss them more than you should. I've known several people like this and no doubt you, dear reader, have too.

Jillie Everhart, the heroine of *The Perfect Soldier,* is one of those people. When I first met her in *Black Sheep P.I.,* I was stunned. She's a composite of many women I know and knew, the kind who appear uncomplicated on the bright, bubbly surface but are made of equal measures of silk and steel underneath. Stephanie, Robin, Nikki, Anna, Marilyn, Camille and Natalie, with a little bit of Carrie Underwood thrown in for flash, and you have Jillie. When she meets the man of her dreams, of course she pursues him full-out. As if she ever did anything any other way!

Pair her up with a man who can't feel emotion, a man who is so lost that he doesn't even realize it, and you have one heck of a story. I couldn't wait to write this book. I hope you enjoy reading it as much as I enjoyed writing it.

Best,

Karen Whiddon

KAREN WHIDDON

The Perfect Soldier

Silhouette®

Romantic

SUSPENSE

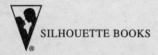

SILHOUETTE BOOKS

Recycling programs
for this product may
not exist in your area.

ISBN-13: 978-0-373-27627-1
ISBN-10:   0-373-27627-3

THE PERFECT SOLDIER

Copyright © 2009 by Karen M. Whiddon

Visit Silhouette Books at www.eHarlequin.com

Printed in U.S.A.

Books by Karen Whiddon

Silhouette Romantic Suspense

One Eye Open #1301
One Eye Closed #1365
Secrets of the Wolf #1397
The Princess's Secret Scandal #1416
Bulletproof Marriage #1484
**Black Sheep P.I. #1513
**The Perfect Soldier #1557

Silhouette Nocturne

*Cry of the Wolf #7
*Touch of the Wolf #12
*Dance of the Wolf #45

Signature Select Collection

*Beyond the Dark
"Soul of the Wolf"

*The Pack
**The Cordasic Legacy

KAREN WHIDDON

started weaving fanciful tales for her younger brothers at the age of eleven. Amidst the Catskill Mountains of New York, then the Rocky Mountains of Colorado, she fueled her imagination with the natural beauty of the rugged peaks and spun stories of love that captivated her family's attention.

Karen now lives in North Texas, where she shares her life with her very own hero of a husband and three doting dogs. Also an entrepreneur, she divides her time between the business she started and writing the contemporary romantic suspense and paranormal romances that readers enjoy. You can e-mail Karen at KWhiddon1@aol.com or write to her at P.O. Box 820807, Fort Worth, TX 76182. Fans of her writing can also check out her Web site, www.KarenWhiddon.com

To Stephanie, Robin, Nikki, Anna, Marilyn, Camille
and Natalie. Some of you have kept in touch.
To the others, I hope you are finding happiness!

Chapter 1

"Commander Cordasic?" The elegantly dressed secretary gave him an impersonal smile tinged with a hint of feminine appreciation. "General Knight will see you now."

Standing, Sebastian Cordasic followed her down a carpeted corridor, back ramrod straight, the starch and perfect fit of his marine uniform both familiar and not.

"Right through here." She indicated a closed door, standing back as he grasped the knob.

When Sebastian entered the room, the general rose to greet him and so did his guest—a woman Sebastian hadn't seen in three months, ever since his brother Dominic had married her sister, Rachel.

Jillie Everhart, international country music superstar and one of the most beautiful women he'd ever met.

What was she doing at the Pentagon in General Knight's office?

Sebastian knew he should have felt a surge of excitement or relief, but he felt absolutely nothing.

"Commander Cordasic?" General Knight was all smiles. "At ease. You know Ms. Everhart, I understand."

Seb tore his gaze away from her. "Yes, sir." Barely allowing his shoulders to relax, he wondered what this was about. Ever since he'd been placed on a mandatory medical leave of absence, he'd been waiting for a summons from General Knight. A summons with new orders, giving him back command of Shadow Unit, the elite, covert unit he'd once lived for. Orders, no matter what they were, where they sent him, that would finally end nearly a year of boredom.

But where did Jillie enter the picture?

General Knight stared at him, as though expecting him to elaborate. Briefly, Seb wondered if the other man was a country music fan. But then why had Seb been invited to their meeting? It didn't make sense.

Jillie made a sound of welcome, low in her graceful, elegant throat. "Seb." Her voice washed over him like honey, soothing and sensual all at once.

When the only move he made to greet her was a slight dip of his chin, she came to him, pressing her curvy body to his, enveloping him in a floral-scented hug.

"How are you?" Her glad cry was followed by an appraising look. "You look good."

Was that a hint of reproach in her dulcet tone? He cast his mind back to when he saw her at Dominic's wedding. She'd made it clear that she was interested in him, but he'd been careful not to promise anything, knowing he couldn't deliver.

He found her attractive, certainly. Desired her, most definitely. But he wasn't in the habit of beginning casual affairs, and a casual affair was all he could give any woman right now.

Besides, a star of Jillie's caliber had her pick of men. Why would she want to mess around with an automaton like him? With her toned curves and mass of long, golden ringlets, she was beautiful enough to have any man she wanted.

General Knight's frown deepened. "You have new orders."

Seb nodded slowly, but wondered why his superior officer had chosen to give him his orders in front of a civilian. "Where to, sir?"

Jillie's grin widened. Her curly blond hair cascaded down her back in bouncy waves. Her hair matched her personality. He'd never met anyone like her—bouncy, bubbly, happy and brimming with life.

Even her choice of clothing reflected her personality. For the occasion—whatever that might be—she'd worn a bright lemon-colored dress. The simple cut of the fabric told him it was probably expensive, no doubt one of those designer labels all the women drooled over.

Again he wondered why she was here.

General Knight cleared his throat. Seb promptly directed his attention back to his superior officer, raising a brow as he waited for the other man to continue.

"We've received new Intel on the same splinter group that held you captive." The general glanced again at Jillie, giving her a faint smile before returning his gaze to Seb.

"Perhaps we should discuss this later, sir?" Seb kept his tone polite. Certainly the general knew better than to let a civvy overhear classified information.

General Knight smiled. "This particular bit of Intel concerns her, too, Commander."

Seb nodded as if he understood, though he didn't really. He didn't see what the bastards who'd made him into an emotionless robot had to do with Jillie and said so.

"We're getting to that." Hands behind his back, General Knight strolled around the bookcase-lined room. With his graying hair and well-toned body, he cut a dapper figure in his uniform.

"They still want you, Commander Cordasic. The capture of a legendary Cordasic was quite a coup for them, and they want you back. What exactly they did to you is still unknown, though we're trying to find out."

If they hadn't found out by now, Seb doubted they ever would. Whatever experiments they'd performed on him had been done while he was unconscious. He'd woken feeling no different than usual—or so he'd thought. Later he realized he felt blank. The desire to escape had completely left him, as had the yearning to rejoin his unit. He felt absolutely nothing—no fury, no regret, no fear.

The worst thing was that he knew what emotions he normally would feel—should feel—and yet he no longer experienced any of them.

Now was no different. Jillie might be delightful eye candy, but she had no more effect on him than anything else.

Again, he focused on the general, waiting to hear the

rest. Hearing that the terrorists wanted him recaptured was not a surprise. Evidently they hadn't yet finished their work on him.

Sebastian might not be able to feel, but he knew one thing with absolute certainty. He'd put a bullet through his own head before he'd allow himself to be recaptured and turned into an even worse monster.

"Intel has intercepted conversations that indicate some members of the splinter cell have vowed to stop at nothing to recapture you and are on the way here. Nothing you care about is safe."

Seb started to say he cared about nothing, but as the impact of General Knight's words hit him, he bit back a curse. "My family?"

"Exactly. We'll notify them to take extra precautions."

"I want them guarded."

"Already done."

Seb nodded. "And Jillie—Ms. Everhart? Is she in danger, too?"

Giving both of them an assessing look, General Knight nodded. "Especially after she posted what she did on her blog."

Jillie's creamy complexion turned tomato-red. "I'm sure once the media picked that up and ran with it, the terrorists figured I'd be a good bet for bait."

He met her gaze blankly. "I have no idea what you're talking about."

Now even the general appeared shocked. Both he and Jillie gave Seb incredulous looks.

"How could you not? It's been all over every tabloid for weeks, not to mention the Internet."

Seb shrugged. "I've been down in the Florida Keys

at a friend's fishing place. No tabloids there. No TV or computer, either. What did you post on your blog?"

Her blush deepened, but she didn't look away. He had to give her credit for that.

"I made the post after I got back from Vegas the first time. After you and Dominic rescued my nephew Cole from that horrible man, I told my fans about what had happened. I told them I'd met you, though I didn't use your full name. I don't know how they figured that out."

"So?" The old Seb would have felt impatience. "What does that have to do with the terrorists?"

She lifted her chin higher. "I told them I thought I had met The One." As she paused for emphasis, her sapphire-blue eyes searched his face, trying to make certain he understood. "You, Seb. I blogged that you were The One."

While Seb tried to process this, General Knight stepped in to finish. "You've become a minor celebrity, son. Jillie Everhart's fiancé."

"I'm not her fiancé."

"You are now." General Knight forestalled Seb's protest with a wave of his hand. "Until this thing is over and we've captured the splinter cell, I want you to act as Jillie's fiancé." He paused for effect. "This is only one part of your orders."

Seb clenched his jaw and jerked his head in a quick nod. "And the rest of them, sir?"

"According to Intel, the splinter cell wants to use Ms. Everhart as bait to capture you." General Knight's mouth tightened, then relaxed into a smile as he looked at Jillie. "The president's a big fan. He wants to make sure that doesn't happen. Your orders are to protect Ms.

Everhart and make sure nothing happens to her. We'll keep an eye on you, and when they make their move, we'll grab them."

From his years in the military, Seb knew protesting would be futile. Still, Jillie was a civilian. He didn't mind being used as bait, but he sure as hell minded them using *her.* At least, he knew he should mind.

"Once we capture them, we can find out what they did to you, son." The general clapped him on the shoulder. "As well as learn how to undo it. You'd like that, wouldn't you?"

General Knight appeared to take Seb's lack of response for assent. "From today on, I want you stuck to Ms. Everhart's side like glue. Where she goes, you go. Her own bodyguards will be replaced by undercover federal agents. You'll step in as team leader."

"The FBI is involved." Seb frowned. "I'd like permission to replace them with my own men."

General Knight shook his head. "Sorry, no can do. You can have a few of your men, of course, but technically the Feds are in charge."

Jillie didn't seem to mind. She smiled sweetly at them both. Too sweetly. He quickly realized what was wrong. She was too quiet. During the time they'd spent together in Vegas, he'd noticed Jillie did everything flamboyantly.

Either Jillie was really worried, or she had something up her sleeve.

His head began to ache. Even before his capture, Seb had preferred to keep things uncomplicated. He was a straightforward kind of guy. All the Cordasics were. It was the way they were wired.

He would have bet Jillie was the same way. She'd been up-front and sincere. He'd felt comfortable around her, able to relax without worrying about underlying meanings and subterfuge.

Her smile widened, making him realize he'd been staring. The fact that she seemed on board with this plan told him she had no idea what she was getting into.

General Knight held out a manila folder. "Everything you need is in here."

Seb took it, dropping his chin in acknowledgment.

"You have two hours." The general consulted his watch. "Go home and pack. Call me in an hour to let me know who you want on your team. I'll make the arrangements to get them to you."

His men. If Seb were the man he used to be, he'd be overjoyed. "Aren't they still in Kuwait?"

The general gave him a sharp look. "Their location is classified. Call me with names. I'll send a driver to pick you up at 1700 hours. Dismissed."

He was no longer considered in the loop—no longer given classified information. Nothing surprised him anymore. Seb turned on his heel, nodded once at Jillie and headed for the door while turning the names of his select unit over in his head and wondering how he'd choose just four.

Jillie watched him go, her chest aching. "He doesn't seem too happy," she commented.

"He's a soldier. He'll do what he's told. Once he thinks about this, he'll realize it's a very good plan."

"You'll keep him safe, right?" Her voice sounded sharp, but she didn't care. Sebastian Cordasic was just too important to her to let the military take chances with his safety. "I don't like the idea of the bad guys coming after him."

The older man gave her a fatherly smile. "Don't worry your pretty little head about that, dear. We marines can take care of our own."

"You'd better," she said darkly and then softened her harsh words with a brilliant—and utterly false—smile. "I think we both agree it would be a public relations disaster if the media were to learn of a botched operation."

This time, General Knight took her words seriously. Narrowing his eyes, he studied her with a flinty stare and then nodded. "It won't be botched. Now if there isn't anything else, I have a meeting to attend. My secretary will show you the way out."

His secretary magically appeared as though she'd been listening at the door. Gliding across the room, she smiled at Jillie. "Ms. Everhart? If you'll follow me."

The general held out his hand. Since Jillie firmly believed in hugging rather than handshakes, she stepped around his outstretched arm and gave him a big hug. He appeared at a loss for words.

Stepping back, Jillie gave him a grin and a jaunty little wave before following the secretary out of the room.

It took Seb all of ten minutes to pack what he needed. After tossing in six dark T-shirts, three pairs of jeans, a week's worth of underwear and socks, and an extra pair of black boots, he zipped his duffel closed. He didn't need much. As long as his trusty Ruger and shoulder harness were in place, he was good to go.

Next he had to choose his men. One was a given—

Ryan Timmons, his second in command. Ryan had led the charge to free Seb from his prison cell in Kuwait. The others weren't so easy, but he eventually settled on Travis Mendenhall, Archie Bell and Charlie Hill. He called the general and gave the names.

Finally, he sat down with a pad of paper and worked out a rudimentary plan of action. Keeping Jillie safe would be easy—as long as he kept her away from the general public. With her occupation, that wouldn't be easy, but based on the elevated level of threat, gaining her full cooperation shouldn't be difficult.

After jotting down the key points, he stuffed the pad into the side pocket of his duffel bag.

He was ready.

The rest of the time he spent pacing the confines of his small, impersonal apartment in Bethesda. He had no plants or pets to worry about, and if the place were to burn to the ground while he was on assignment, he'd lose very little. The apartment had come furnished with a ragtag couch, a wobbly kitchen table, and a bed with a saggy mattress. The few personal belongings—some books, CDs and a flat-screen television—were easily replaceable and gave no hints about him.

Seb didn't care. He viewed the place as just somewhere to sleep and wait for his next assignment, not as a home to make comfortable and entertain in. Men like him didn't have friends outside their unit, and ever since he'd been freed from prison in Kuwait, the only kind of lover he'd taken had been the kind he'd picked up in a bar. Sexual desire had been the one thing they hadn't taken from him, maybe because it was a bodily urge rather than an emotion.

The military driver arrived promptly at 1700 hours, pulling into the parking lot in a car so nondescript it had to be a government vehicle.

Stepping outside into the late afternoon heat, Seb locked the door and pocketed the keys. He took the steps down two at a time, back and shoulders straight, head held high.

The driver flashed ID and Seb got into the car. While the other man drove, Seb took the opportunity to study the folder the general had given him. As usual, the only thing of real import was his orders, and those said precious little. Closing the file, he shoved it into the side pocket of his duffel and settled back for the drive.

They pulled up to the private airport just outside D.C. at the same time as a long, black Lincoln limo. The instant Seb's car rolled to a stop, he jumped out, striding across the pavement and beating the limo driver to the back door.

He pulled open the door. When no one emerged, he peered inside. Jillie had one hand under her heart-shaped face and lay stretched out on the backseat, sound asleep.

He stared for a moment, unable to look away. Finally, the driver behind him cleared his throat and Seb snapped out of his trance or whatever.

"Jillie." His voiced sounded like sandpaper. He swallowed hard and tried again. "Jillie, wake up. We're here."

A slow smile spread across her face. "Seb," she murmured, stretching. With a delicate yawn, she opened her eyes, the vibrant blue warmth sending a shock to his gut. Hell, she was beautiful. If he weren't half a man...

Seb grimaced, stepping back from the car. They'd

pulled up in front of a gleaming Gulfstream G350. He'd
bet the aircraft had a price tag upward of twenty million.
Taking a long look at it, he whistled. "I had no idea mu-
sicians, even ones as popular as you, made enough
money to afford a private jet like this."

Jumping out of the limo, she laughed, the lighthearted sound skittering over his skin like a whisper of
cool air. "Oh, it's not mine. It belongs to the record
label. Under these circumstances, they insisted I use it."

"They must really like you."

"Maybe." She caught her lip with her teeth. "They
didn't want me flying commercial when there are terrorists out to get me."

He tore his gaze away from her flushed face and
tousled hair. "Good point," he rasped, wondering what
was wrong with him. She'd had a similar effect on him
in Vegas, making him react when he didn't feel like he
was going to, as if his subconscious was taking over for
his missing emotions.

She led the way up the steps into the jet. Inside,
cream-colored leather seats and polished teak accents
exuded luxury. Jillie took a seat next to a built-in desk
and he sat across from her, dropping his duffel onto the
chair next to him.

The preflight check went smoothly. A uniformed
hostess materialized and asked if they wanted anything
to drink. Seb opted for coffee and Jillie asked for hot
tea. The woman promised to bring the drinks after they
took off and promptly disappeared.

Once they were in the air, the hostess made good on
her promise, serving Seb a large mug of hot, black
coffee. Once Jillie got her tea, she squeezed lemon into

the cup, curled her legs under her and sipped her drink with an expression of contentment.

After watching her for a moment, Seb reached into his bag and retrieved the papers he'd worked on earlier. "I thought we needed to have a plan," he said, keeping his tone brusque and businesslike. "I'd like to make this situation as safe for you as possible—"

"While maximizing the effectiveness of using you as bait," she finished for him. "You'd like to get this over with as quickly as possible."

He stared. "Of course. Don't you?"

"Of course." Despite her soft smile, she sounded as if she were mimicking him. "So what's your plan?"

Glancing at his list, he began reading. "No public appearances. It'd be better if we stay in one place, somewhere with good security that I can monitor."

"Won't work." Her soft interruption came in a velvety voice cloaked in steel. "I have concerts, two awards shows I've got to attend, and several appearances booked. I can't cancel those."

"But—"

"Let me put this another way. I *won't* cancel." Shifting in her chair, she drank the last of her tea, setting down the cup with a decisive click. "You'll have to come up with another plan. I can give you a detailed list of my schedule. You'll need to work around that."

Seb was dumbfounded. Apparently Jillie had no idea of the risk she was facing. He gave the only response he could think of. "Does General Knight know about this?"

To his disbelief, she laughed. "I don't know. Honestly Seb, I don't really care. I don't work for him. I'm not giving up my life and disappointing all my fans for

the sake of a military operation. The president asked
General Knight to keep me safe. The general contacted
you. If y'all want your plan to work, you'll have to plot
it around my schedule."

Just as he was about to frame a retort, Seb froze as
the plane dropped twenty feet and the cabin lights went
black.

Chapter 2

Jillie bit down on her bottom lip so hard it hurt, but she didn't scream or launch herself at Seb, though she wanted his strong arms around her, protecting her, and his deep, calm voice telling her everything would be all right.

Closing her eyes tight, she bowed her head and muttered a quick prayer.

As the jet leveled out and the cabin lights came back on she opened her eyes. Her gaze caught Seb's and the calm reassurance she saw in his brown eyes made her breathe a sigh of relief.

A moment later the pilot's voice came over the intercom, apologizing for the turbulence and advising them to keep their seat belts on for the time being.

"That was scary." She hated that she sounded a bit

breathless, but her racing heartbeat had barely begun
to slow.

Seb nodded. Staring hard at her, he held up his paper.
"Jillie, if you think that was bad, let me tell you, that
was nothing compared to what could happen with these
terrorists."

As she started to speak, he lifted his hand to forestall her. "Please. Think about this before you decide
anything. Don't make rash decisions. So what if you
cancel a few concerts? You can reschedule them once
this is over. It'll be difficult—no, damn near impossible—to keep you protected up there on stage."

"I'm not going to disappoint my fans."

"Won't it disappoint them more if you die?"

"If anyone can protect me, you can." She spoke with
absolute confidence, refusing to let him see he'd shocked
her. Even if she turned out to be wrong about Seb being
The One, she knew he wouldn't let anything happen to her.

"Why do you say that?" He dragged his hand through
his hair in apparent frustration.

How could she put into words what she knew—
what she *felt*—deep down in her gut? Seb might not be
able to feel—a condition she hoped was only tempo-
rary—but she'd known seconds after spending time
with him in Vegas that he wasn't the type of man to let
anyone else down no matter what the cost to himself.
He'd proved that by helping Dominic save her nephew
from a madman and providing support to Rachel in her
time of need.

Because she could say none of this, she settled for
the obvious. "General Knight told me about the Cordasic legacy."

"He did, did he?" Seb looked blank, but he actually sounded displeased.

"Yes. Of course, Rachel mentioned it in passing, when we were all in Vegas. I think it's amazing how your family has continued the tradition down through the centuries. The general told me about your ancestors—Thomas Cordasic in the Revolutionary War, Beareguard Cordasic in the Civil War, and so on. General Knight said the Cordasics are known among the international spy community for breeding the best undercover agents."

The more she talked, the more uncomfortable Seb appeared. He ran a finger around the inside of his collar, as though his shirt was too tight.

"He said your family has served in the CIA, FBI, Navy SEALS, and many other covert military organizations, and that failure is never an option with you."

A muscle worked in his jaw, but still he said nothing, merely nodding to show agreement with her words.

Pleased, she sat back. Any time she succeeded in ruffling Seb's unflappable cool, she felt she'd made progress in helping him to feel.

"You know Dom's story," he cautioned. "When he was a hostage negotiator for the FBI, his partner got killed and Dom lost his job. Even though he did everything right, mistakes happen."

The jet hit another round of turbulence, bouncing Jillie up and then slamming her hard against the window. A small cry escaped her as her head slammed into the hard fiberglass.

Instantly, Seb came to her, kneeling beside her seat. She hadn't even heard him unbuckle his seat belt.

"Are you all right?" Cupping her chin with one hand,

he felt along the back of her head with the other and massaged her scalp. Proving yet again that she was right about him and his ability to protect her.

This time, the sound that escaped her was one of pleasure. She let herself drift, eyes half-closed, unwilling to speak and have him stop touching her.

"Jillie? Answer me." His sharp tone told her she had to respond.

She opened her eyes to find his face mere inches from her own. If she were brave, exceptionally brave, or maybe just foolhardy, she would lean forward and touch her lips to his. She shivered at the thought.

Though she didn't consider herself a coward, Jillie wasn't a fool, either. As she gazed into his beautiful amber-brown eyes, she knew that to kiss him now would be a huge mistake.

"I'm fine." Her mouth was suddenly dry, and she licked her lips, gratified at the way his gaze followed the small movement.

He pushed himself to his feet, uncoiling his muscular body with inherent grace. Aching, she watched him make his way across the small aisle to his own seat and kept watching while he buckled himself back in. Unable to look away, she summoned a small smile as he met her gaze and lifted a brow in question. "Are you sure?"

"Yes. Thanks for caring." She kept her gaze locked with his. "We should be in Boulder in a few hours. I don't know about you, but I'm going to try and get some sleep."

Staring right back, he finally nodded. "Good idea. We can talk more later."

Finally, she could let the exhaustion that had been dogging her all day take over. Ron, her manager, had phoned her in the middle of a grueling, forty-seven-city tour and asked her to fly to Washington to speak with General Knight. Because curiosity was a huge part of her nature and since the summons had come at the beginning of her four-day break, she'd immediately complied.

Now, though, she needed to rest. In between shows, she had a little ritual she'd come to swear by. Sebastian would probably find green tea, scented candles, daily affirmations and tantric chants distasteful, but she had no intention of trying to pretend to be something she was not. Not even for him.

Especially not for him. He could take her as she was or not at all.

She drifted off to sleep, dreaming of her much-missed yoga workout.

"Jillie, we're here. Wake up." Seb's voice was perfectly masculine—low and growly with a touch of sin. As a musician, she'd always been a sucker for voices, and found it interesting that the sound so seldom matched the speaker.

Seb was one of the rare exceptions.

Covering her mouth as a yawn escaped her, she took her time stretching before opening her eyes. Even without looking, she felt his gaze on her, burning like a brand. He might pretend the attraction wasn't mutual, but her female intuition knew better.

She enjoyed the way he watched her.

As the jet circled, preparing to descend, she sat up straight in her seat, tidied her clothes, and began fussing with her hair.

"You look fine," Seb growled. "Leave it."

Startled, she blinked. "Was that a compliment?"

His dark expression was at war with his words. He shrugged. "Take it however you want. I just wanted to let you know your hair was okay."

She hid her smile. By the time this tour was over, she hoped Seb would think she looked more than fine.

Turning his head, he tried to peer out the window at the dark sky. "I don't see airport lights yet. Are we landing at DIA?"

"Denver International? No. We're using Centennial. It's a smaller airport in Englewood and a lot easier to get in and out of."

As the crew prepared for landing, she felt his gaze on her again. Slowly, she turned her head. "Is something wrong?"

"No." He shook his head. "I need to check in with my family and let them know what's going on. They're sure to notice the guys General Knight said he sent, no matter how unobtrusive they're supposed to be."

"I see no need to worry Dom and Rachel. They just bought their first home together. Let them enjoy it."

"Jillie, these are international terrorists. People with big money behind them. The threat is very real. Do you honestly want your family to learn about this from the media rather than you?"

"The media?" Her sharp tone matched his. "They've already gone nuts over our supposed engagement. But they can't know about this. You were—are—Covert Ops. Surely you know how to keep things under wraps."

He went completely still, his hard gaze pinning her. "How do you know I'm Covert Operations?"

"Come on. We're practically family. Your brother knows and so does my sister. I'm sure one of them probably told me. Don't worry." She gave him a wide smile, inviting him to reciprocate. He didn't.

The jet touched down smoothly. Still feeling fuzzy-headed from sleep—or lack of it—Jillie dug her cell phone out of her bag. While the pilot maneuvered them down the pavement to the private hangar, she sent a text message to her driver.

"What was that?" Though he asked the question in a casual tone, Seb's sharp gaze watched her phone. A second later, the message tone sounded. Her driver had arrived and would be waiting at the hangar.

"My driver is ready for us." Stowing the phone back in her bag, she suppressed a sigh. "You know what? I'm not the enemy here."

He slowly nodded. "You're right. My apologies."

Though she watched him closely, she had no idea what he was thinking or feeling. Or *if* he was feeling. In any other man, she might put his sudden testiness down to nerves.

Once the jet stopped, the hostess and the pilot opened the doors.

"Stay here until I secure the area."

Jillie did, admiring his broad shoulders and narrow hips as he left the plane. Finally, with a sweep of his hand, Seb indicated Jillie should join him. She did, enjoying inhaling her first breath of the dry mountain air. Though she had a house in Nashville—practically a requirement for a country music artist—her eclectic converted barn nestled in the foothills of the Rockies was her true home.

With Seb's solid presence close beside her, she felt an overwhelming sense of contentment. Her friends—especially the more jaded ones—constantly teased her about what they called her romantic fantasies, but she couldn't change the way she felt nor did she want to. How could she sing heartfelt love songs if she didn't believe in the power of love?

Right now, with this man, she couldn't help but feel everything would work out. She cast Seb a grin, ignoring his frown, and practically danced the few feet across the pavement to her waiting car.

Following an almost giddy Jillie made Seb feel as close to furious as he'd felt since returning from Kuwait. Though they'd hung out a little in Vegas, he had no idea she was so innocent. Was it an act? She and Rachel were twins, and he couldn't understand how their personalities could be so dissimilar.

Introverted Rachel and flamboyant, full-of-life Jillie were like night and day. In Vegas he'd often felt like a moth, drawn to Jillie's flame but keeping a safe distance, knowing if he got too close, he'd go up in a puff of black smoke.

He'd known this, known, too, his body's reaction to her warm-hearted sexuality. Seb anticipated having to keep his always-active libido in check—he'd done so before and would do so again.

But Jillie's absolute refusal to face reality had him floored. How could an international recording artist be so naive?

If he was going to run this operation the same way he'd run the Shadow Unit, he needed absolute obedience to his orders and instant compliance with his plan—not laughter and arch looks.

Once they were enclosed in the backseat of her limo and the driver had pulled away from the hangar, Seb tried again. "Since you don't want to hear my ideas, why don't you tell me yours?"

She blinked at him in the dimly lit car, then her delectable mouth curved in a smile. "My ideas? Simple. I do what I normally do and you and your people catch the bad guys. I don't need to know the details."

"Why not?" he asked, before he could help himself.

"Because I don't want to worry about you, Seb. If I'm worried, I might make mistakes."

She caught her lip in her teeth, a move he noticed she did quite often. "You know, sometimes this whole music thing seems like a house of cards to me," she said. "One false move, one card pulled away, and the whole thing comes tumbling down."

Jillie had two platinum albums and had just released her third, but when he pointed this out to her, she simply shook her head. "Sheer luck. In this industry, you have one flop and they're already pushing you aside in the search for the next big thing."

Still, he didn't see what any of that had to do with the threat to them both. "Let me get this straight. You're worried about your career?"

"And you're worried about the terrorists."

"Jillie—"

"You're doing your job and I'm doing mine."

He sighed, deciding to humor her a little. "If only things were that simple."

"They are, if you don't make them complicated."

In her world, maybe. Not in his.

As they drove northwest on the highway, the lights flashing past gave him glimpses of her beautiful, heart-shaped face.

Leaning back against the seat, she'd closed her eyes. "Do you mind if I sleep again? It's about forty-five minutes to my house."

The large back area of the limo suddenly seemed too confining, though Seb didn't understand why. "No problem," he answered, knowing it would be a long time before he slept. He didn't mind. After the experiments, he'd found he didn't need as much sleep. Sometimes four hours a night was more than enough.

Long after her even breathing told him she'd fallen asleep, Seb watched her. Adaptability to all conditions was one of the Shadow Unit's specialties. Dealing with Jillie would be a challenge, but no matter what problems her cavalier attitude might present, he and his guys would figure out a way to overcome them.

Right now some of his best men were on their way to Boulder. If he'd been able to feel, Seb knew he'd be overjoyed to see them again. Over the years they'd worked together they'd functioned as a well-oiled machine. They'd built trust, respect and a camaraderie that he sorely missed. These guys had been part of the rescue operation that freed him from his prison cell. Though Seb had been whisked away and hadn't seen them again, he knew they'd saved his life, if not his sanity.

He looked forward to thanking them for that.

With each curve of the road they climbed higher. Highway 36 went right into Boulder, where it became Twenty-eighth Street. As they continued driving parallel to the mountains, the lights became brighter and more numerous.

Seb glanced behind them periodically, trying to see if they were being followed. Traffic was light, and every time he began to suspect someone was tailing them, the car turned off or dropped too far behind to be a concern.

Judging by the number of turns the limo made, Seb bet the driver had been instructed to make sure they weren't followed. Either that or there was no direct route to Jillie's house.

He wondered what kind of house Jillie owned and why she'd chosen Boulder. Her family, like his, came from Texas.

Though he'd never been to Boulder, he'd seen pictures. He could see how the pastoral setting and eclectic energy would appeal to an artist. Yet even though there'd been several magazine articles on Jillie Everhart and her Nashville home had been featured on some TV show, he hadn't heard about the house in Boulder. He hoped it was some huge, brick fortress perched high on a hill and surrounded by a wrought-iron fence. A fenced estate would make it easier to defend Jillie.

He had no doubt that he was going to have to defend her. Although he didn't remember much about his captors, he knew once they set their mind to something, they moved swiftly and without hesitation. He only hoped the terrorists didn't act before his team arrived.

After what seemed another ten or twelve more random turns on tree-lined streets, they finally pulled up to a house.

Oblivious, Jillie still slept.

Squinting out at total darkness, Seb opened his door

cautiously and stepped out, scanning the scene for any hint of danger. Illuminated in the moonlight, glowing a soft, ghostly white, a restored, two-story farmhouse sat nestled among towering evergreens and willowy aspen trees.

The home was utterly unpretentious. There was even a white picket fence surrounding the tidy front yard.

Unpretentious and homey. And, now that he thought about it, exactly Jillie. Underneath all the glitter and glamour, she seemed a country girl at heart.

Like her, the house was beautiful and, for some odd reason, merely looking at it made his chest hurt.

With one hand over his heart, he stared up at the house. Though he'd never been to Boulder, he felt as if he'd been here before, right at this spot. He could imagine the way the house looked in the winter, welcoming yellow light spilling from windows onto the snow, a curl of fragrant smoke drifting up from the chimney. He saw a dog, too, with a full black and white coat, running down the front sidewalk to greet him.

A memory? Not possible, as he knew without a doubt he'd never seen this place before. This was probably another strange result of one of those awful experiments. Because he didn't have time to dwell on it now, he filed the memory/reaction away for future reflection.

"Do you have a key?" Turning to the startled driver, who'd also gotten out of the car, Seb held out a hand. "I'd like to go inside and secure the place before she wakes up."

"No need." Jillie's soft voice came from behind him. He turned to find her standing, swaying slightly in the cool mountain breeze. "I have an alarm system—my manager insisted I put it in, even though there's no need here."

"Let me go first anyway," he insisted. "Just to be safe."

"It's safe. We're safe." Pushing past him, she weaved through the small picket fence gate and up the side-walk. "I have lights, but they're not on since I've been gone awhile." Even half-asleep, her husky voice sounded cheerful.

Catching up to her, Seb took hold of her arm. "You need protection. Let me do my job."

At the carved front door they paused. She ran her slender hand lovingly over the polished wood, giving him a soft, wistful smile.

"When I first saw this house, I swore I could hear echoes of its history, of the past. Though it was empty when I looked at it, I could almost hear children's laughter and tiny footsteps running. I could picture the furniture—where it would be placed, exactly what kind—and when I walked into the dining room, I saw a huge table set for twenty, groaning under the weight of a feast. I knew then that I'd come home. I didn't haggle over the price and I bought the house the same day."

"How long have you owned it?"

"A year now. I bought it after my second record went platinum." She brushed her long hair out of her eyes and handed him the key. Seb opened the door, alert for any movement.

Immediately, a loud beeping sounded. "My alarm. I have sixty seconds to punch in my code, or the police are called. Let's go inside."

He nodded, clearing his throat, which still ached, and followed her into the foyer. He watched as the limo driver placed their bags inside then said good night. "How many bedrooms?"

"Three, why?"

"My team will be here tonight. They'll need a room to use. They can bunk down together."

She flicked on a light and began punching her code into a white keypad mounted on the wall. "I haven't got around to buying spare beds yet."

"No need." He couldn't help but smile at the consternation he saw on her face. "They're used to much rougher conditions."

"You expect them to sleep on the *floor?*" Her bright blue eyes clouded over. "No way."

"We can talk about this tomorrow." He felt exposed standing there, silhouetted by the light she'd turned on. Outside, the limo began backing down the driveway.

He watched as Jillie closed the front door and clicked the deadbolt. She reset the alarm and turned to him. "Let me give you a tour."

His cell phone rang. "Cordasic."

"Hey, chief." It was Ryan Timmons, senior member of his team. "We're about an hour away."

"Excellent. I should be done securing the location by then." As he spoke, he registered the way Jillie arched her brows in surprise.

"One problem. Archie couldn't make it."

Seb took a moment to digest this news. "What do you mean, couldn't make it? He got orders, didn't he?"

"He's…" Ryan's voice cracked. "In the hospital. We don't know if he's going to make it or not."

Seb cursed his lack of emotion about the loss of a valuable team mate and friend. "What happened?"

"Sniper. Came out of nowhere. Got him and Smith."

Smith was the electronics expert. Seb had briefly considered making him part of the team, but hadn't seen the need for his particular specialty.

"They've been flown to Ramstein. We've been assured they're getting the best care."

Swallowing hard, Seb searched for the right words. Ryan would want and expect reassurance from his commander, and Seb was determined to give it despite his lack of emotion. "I'm sorry. They're both good men. Fighters. They'll make it."

"Yeah." Another moment passed while Ryan paid silent homage to his comrades. When he spoke again, his tone was different, more businesslike. "What kind of move do you expect from the cell?"

Seb found himself wishing for a smoke for the first time in six months. "I wish I knew. We've got to be prepared for anything."

"At least you know they won't kill you." Though Ryan joked, he was serious, too. "They want you too bad for that. When we were briefed, we were told they said they'll stop at nothing to get you back. So, what's the plan?"

"We're to protect Jillie Everhart."

"Your *fiancée?* I can't wait to hear all about this one."

"Long story," Seb said in order to forestall answering any further questions in front of Jillie. "I'll brief you fully once you arrive. Text me when you're in town."

As he closed the phone, a loud crash came from the top floor.

Chapter 3

Jillie froze. "I don't know—"

"Don't move." Right in front of her eyes, Seb seemed to become someone else. Someone dangerous, lethal. Her eyes widened as she realized he had a gun.

Jillie hated guns, but she had to concede that in this situation a weapon might be necessary.

"No one can get in my house," she said. "I have an alarm system. You heard it beeping."

"Windows?"

"They're alarmed, too. I also have motion sensors." She started for the light switch at the base of the stairs.

"Jillie, wait." He grabbed her arm. "Leave the lights off. I'm going up. Stay here while I check that out."

She shivered at his touch. He glanced sharply at her and she knew he thought her trembling was from fear.

"I want to go with you," she said.

He muttered something about needing backup to watch over her. She latched on to that.

"You shouldn't leave me alone."

"True." His hard gaze raked over her. "But I shouldn't take you with me, either." Considering, he finally jerked his chin. "Come on. We're going up. You stay right behind me."

"Okay."

"Right behind me," he repeated. "Are you ready?"

She nodded, her heart pounding despite her certainty that no one could have gotten into her home undetected.

But what had caused the sound?

Slowly, they moved up the curved staircase, keeping close to the wall. As usual, the step third from the top gave off a loud creak.

Seb froze, glancing back at her. She shrugged, wishing she'd had the presence of mind to warn him in advance.

After a moment's pause, they continued.

When they reached the landing, Seb crouched, motioning her to do the same.

"Where's your bedroom?" he whispered. Jillie pointed to the right. She stayed as close to him as she could as they crept across the landing.

They made it to her room safely and, as they moved through the doorway, Jillie caught her breath. She'd left her blinds open and moonlight spilled silver into the room, highlighting her huge four-poster bed.

Hyperconscious of Seb standing in front of her, she tried to breathe normally. Her breasts and belly tightened and her heart raced. How many times had she tossed and turned in that same bed, aching with wanting him? Ever since she'd met Sebastian Cordasic, there'd been no other man for her.

"The windows all look secure." Oblivious to her arousal, Seb moved around the room, inspecting everything. He circled her bed, peered underneath, then headed toward her walk-in closet.

Swallowing hard, she followed.

"I don't know what could have made that noise." He flicked on the closet light, then whistled. "This is as big as most people's bedrooms."

"I know." She grinned at him, unrepentant. "It's one of the things I love about this house."

He strolled down the wall of clothing racks, brushing items aside to check out between and under them. His large, strong hands looked tan and completely out of place on her delicate silk and sparkly sequins.

He paused when he got to her shoes, but he inspected them without comment. Maybe he already knew a woman couldn't ever have too many shoes.

After completely circling her closet, he headed toward her bathroom. She stared after him, wondering how just being in the same room with him could have such a strong effect on her libido.

"Jillie, come here." Seb stood at the side of her brand-new, marble whirlpool tub.

She hurried over. Her oversize brass candlestick had fallen into the tub, no doubt the source of the crash. But not the cause.

"Look."

A baby squirrel tried valiantly to escape from the tub.

But each time it leaped for the side, its tiny feet couldn't gain purchase on the slippery marble, and it fell back to the bottom.

"There's your intruder."

"If there's a baby, there's a mother somewhere nearby, right?"

He started off. "We've got to find the nest."

Grabbing his arm, she made him look at her. "No killing. We need to trap them and set them free outside."

He glanced from her fingers, which were pale against his tanned arm, to her face. "Do you have a trap?"

Pulling her hand away, she slowly shook her head. "No. Can't you call animal control? Won't they come get them?"

"We don't want strangers coming here."

She looked again at the baby squirrel. The tiny thing still tried to escape the tub. "Where do you suppose its mother is?"

"Probably in your attic. I'll check it out. If there is a mother squirrel there, we're going to need something to use as a cage. I can get a baby out without too much trouble, but a full-grown squirrel is a different matter."

"Let me call my next-door neighbor. He might have a trap."

Her quick phone call solved the problem. Eugene, her neighbor's son, promised to bring over their humane trap.

After she showed Seb the attic stairs, Jillie went downstairs to make some hot tea. The doorbell rang. As she headed toward the door, Seb came racing down the stairs, blocking her.

"Wait," he said. "Let me."

"But it's probably only—"

"Jillie, I'm here to protect you." His no-nonsense tone thrilled her despite herself. "Let me do my job."

She stepped aside, hovering in the sitting room while he answered the door.

It was Eugene with the trap. Seb thanked him and promised to return it shortly.

While Seb set the trap, she went back to the kitchen only to find that her hot tea had gotten cold. Exhaustion set in and, too tired to even microwave her mug, she carried the drink into the living room and sat on her favorite chair.

A few minutes later, Seb joined her. "Trap's set."

She nodded. "What'd you do with the baby?"

"Herded him into the trap and carried him back to the nest. It's in the eaves just outside one of the attic windows. I didn't see any other babies. They'd chewed a hole in the wall between the closet and the attic, which explains how they got in. I blocked it up."

She liked the sound of his voice. Listening to him talk made her feel secure. Snuggling deeper into her chair, she didn't bother to try and make conversation. She knew Seb would understand.

Though she tried to stay awake, Jillie's amazing blue eyes kept drifting closed. Seb watched her long lashes flutter as she struggled to focus on him while he talked. Deliberately, he'd spoken in a low, expressionless tone, droning on and on until he thought even he might become comatose.

She nodded in all the right places, flashed him a tired smile or two, and listened. It was a testament to her extraordinary will that she managed to stay awake as long as she did.

Finally she'd lost her battle and fell asleep sitting up, with her long legs curled beneath her.

So beautiful. Easily the loveliest woman he'd ever known, and he'd known plenty. Yet Jillie was more than a heart-shaped face and full mouth, more than eyes the color of sapphires. While her lush curves would tempt a saint to sin, her vitality attracted people. Most people's life force was a mere spark, but hers was a blazing inferno. Even if he'd been a normal man with emotions and feelings—*especially* if he'd been normal—Seb suspected he'd get burned if he got too close to her.

He'd have to be content to appreciate her from a safe distance. It appeared he'd been freed from one prison only to be forced to live in another.

While he watched her, his cell phone quietly rang. Glad he'd turned the volume down, Seb got up and went into the foyer. He looked at the displayed number and shook his head. Lea. He hadn't talked to his sister since Dom and Rachel's wedding. He hoped she wasn't calling to tell him their grandfather had died. The elderly man had hovered on death's door for months now, but every time some doctor started thinking the eightysomething-year-old was about to expire, Phillip Cordasic rallied.

"Hey, lil' sis." Though he couldn't actually feel grief, Seb nonetheless braced himself for the bad news. "How's Phillip?"

"He's fine." She chuckled. "Hello to you, too, and yes, I'm fine. Thanks for asking."

"I'm sorry. I was worried about Grandfather."

"Apology accepted. Grandpa Phillip's in one of his good but belligerent stages. Yesterday he demanded barbecued spareribs for lunch. When the nurse told him the hospital didn't have them, he threw such a fit that she finally called me. I brought him some from Rusty's."

Typical.

"Grandfather's not why I called," Lea continued. "When were you planning to tell me and Mama that you got engaged?"

Seb groaned. Because this was a top-secret operation, he couldn't tell his family the truth. "Soon."

"The news has been all over the papers for three weeks!" Despite her indignation, hurt also rang in her voice. "Mama said to wait for you to call, but come on, Seb. This is ridiculous. We're your family! Just because we're in Dallas and you're wherever you happen to be at the moment, doesn't mean we've stopped caring about each other."

He swallowed. "Jillie and I are still working on some…issues." There, that'd give Lea something to chew on. Women liked words like that. Though he knew if Lea thought about it, she'd realize Seb would never in a million years say something like what he'd just said.

As he'd suspected she might, she overlooked that fact.

"Issues?" Her soft voice turned sharp. "Jillie Everhart is one of my favorite singers. She's going to be performing at the American Airlines Center here on Friday night. I would have gone, but I have to work." She took a deep breath, then continued. "After I met her at Dom's wedding, I realized she was also one of the nicest, most genuine people I've ever met. Sebastian, if you hurt her, I'll find you and hurt you myself."

Great. Just what he needed—his little she-cat of a sister coming after him. Lea Cordasic might only stand five feet tall, but with her various black belts in martial arts and her skill with a firearm, she was a double menace.

"Are you listening?" she accused him, her own voice tinged with amusement. "I swear, Seb—" Breaking off, she went abruptly quiet. When she continued, she spoke in barely a whisper. "You're getting better, aren't you?"

"You're the second person to ask me that question in as many days," he drawled. "Honestly, the more people ask me that, the more confused I get."

"You didn't answer me."

"You're not listening to what I said."

"I heard you and I'm choosing to ignore you. Are you getting better, Seb?"

"Honest answer? I don't know. Sometimes I think I feel a glimmer of…something. But then it's gone."

Another moment of quiet passed while she digested this. "Will you tell me the minute you do know?"

"Sure," he lied. If and when he ever started becoming normal, the last thing he'd need was his sister peppering him with questions. It was ironic. Once he would have preferred to be this way, knowing a machine made a better soldier. But being captured had shaken that belief. He wasn't sure he wanted to be a perfect soldier any more.

"Excellent. Now, tell me about Jillie. How did this get so serious, so quickly?"

Crap.

"You met her at Dom's wedding. You saw how beautiful she is." All true, so far. As long as Lea didn't press him for specifics, he would be okay. He hated lying to family and would usually simply say the information they wanted was classified. Normally that was enough.

His phone beeped, telling him he had a text message. "Listen, sis, I've got to go. I'll call you again soon."

While she was sputtering something about not being finished, he disconnected the call.

The text message was from Ryan. As instructed, he let Seb know they'd reached the outskirts of Boulder. Quietly, Seb pushed himself up from his chair and went to the front window to wait.

Ryan cut his lights as soon as he turned into the drive. Unwilling to wake Jillie just yet, Seb watched as his men piled out of the Jeep. He waited until they'd started up the walk before he opened the front door.

Silent, moving as though under sniper fire, they hurried inside.

"Hey," Seb said softly, grabbing first Ryan, then the other two men for a quick, arm-around-the-shoulder guy hug.

Ryan cursed, then grinned. "You look good, Commander."

Still carrying their duffels, both Travis and Charlie glanced around.

"Where is she?" Travis asked, looking a little awestruck, an amazing thing on the rugged face of a man used to dodging land mines while desert winds sent sand bullets that stung the eyes.

It dawned on Seb that he'd managed to forget Jillie was a celebrity to the rest of the world.

"Jillie?" Keeping his voice low, Seb pointed and said, "She fell asleep. She's really tired."

"I can't believe we're guarding her," Charlie mused. "I have all of her music on my iPod."

"Me, too." Travis looked excited. "I'm kind of nervous about meeting her."

Seb laughed, earning surprised looks from his men. He didn't know who was more shocked, them or him. "You ought to see you guys. Decorated combat veterans, elite military machines. And you're *nervous?*"

As his face turned nearly as red as his hair, Charlie looked down, moving his foot to scuff the floor as though he were still standing in the desert. At the last moment, he pulled back, not wanting to mark the polished wood with his large boot.

"It's not every day a soldier gets to meet a music star," he mumbled. "Sorry."

Seb clapped him on the back. "Don't be. I'm only kidding."

All three of his men stared, wearing identical expressions of shock. "We heard you couldn't—" Charlie began only to be shushed by the others.

"Sorry, man," Ryan said.

"It's okay. I know what he meant."

Before he'd been taken prisoner, Seb used to joke around with his men. He hadn't known how to joke after the experiments, as they'd heard.

Until now.

"You're getting better." Ryan's dark gaze searched his face. "Have you told the big brass?"

Seb shook his head, unwilling to discuss anything until he himself could process it. "Come on, men. Let me wake up our charge and find out about our quarters. It's late and we all need to get some shut-eye."

As he turned to head back toward the living room, Jillie appeared in the doorway. With her tousled hair and rumpled clothing, she had the look of a woman who'd just been thoroughly made love to.

His body responded. He fervently hoped the other men didn't have the same reaction, because then he'd have to—

Have to what? Fight them? Seb shook his head, wondering that the hell was wrong with him. He'd known the terrorists had short-circuited his brain, but he hadn't been this messed up since Vegas. As a matter of fact, he'd booked the cabin in the Keys to have time alone to reflect on what exactly happened in Vegas.

When Seb had traveled there to help his brother, Dom, and Jillie's sister, Rachel, Jillie and Seb had become pals. The easy camaraderie between them had stunned Seb at first, but he'd gone with the flow, choosing to focus on helping Dom while Jillie tried to help Rachel.

When the situation got intense, as murder investigations often do, Jillie had made no secret of her desire for Seb. Pushing away his own physical attraction, he'd told her he never mixed business and pleasure. Dom and Rachel had told Jillie about Seb's capture and the awful experiments the terrorists had performed on him, resulting in his being completely unable to feel.

Anything. Anything at all.

His situation had made the draw Jillie had for him more than surprising, and even more compelling. He'd resisted, not wanting to hurt her and cause her brilliant smile to dim.

Yet in Vegas, he'd noticed the first cracks in the terrorist's programming. He'd suspected that had a lot to do with Jillie.

He'd finally given up attempting to analyze it, putting everything down to the unusual circumstances. After the killer had been captured, Rachel's son rescued, and Dom and Rachel had gotten back together, Dom's private investigation firm had flourished.

"Hey, guys." Jillie flashed her trademark smile as she crossed the foyer. "I'm so glad you could make it."

The three men cast bemused looks at Seb, but held their silence. He knew none of them would tell her that as soldiers they had no choice in the matter.

Jillie took Seb's arm, sending a shock straight through him. "Come on. Let me show you the rest of the rooms. There are two guestrooms, but they're both unfurnished. I can buy beds tomorrow, once the stores open, but right now—"

"Jillie." Placing his hand over her small one, Seb gave a light squeeze. "Don't worry about that. You don't need to go buy furniture. We'll be fine. I promise."

Glancing down at his hand on hers, no doubt noting his was twice the size of hers, she closed her mouth. Bringing her gaze back to his face, finally she nodded. "So you said. I guess you're right, especially since we have to leave soon for Dallas. I'm playing Dallas Friday night, Houston Saturday and San Antonio on Sunday. After that, we fly to Florida. There are two shows in Miami."

Again the men all looked at one other, carefully avoiding eye contact with Seb. No matter, he knew what they were thinking. Tour? Suppressing a sigh, he realized he had some explaining to do, which was another first. Every previous mission had thrust them right in the middle of a bad spot, and they'd had to fight their way out. There'd been no time for reflection or questions. Simple survival, nothing more, nothing less.

Jillie's lovely blue eyes were slightly clouded with sleep, and she let her gaze touch on each man before letting it linger on Seb. Then, still holding on to Seb's arm, she led the way to the stairway.

Seb glanced back to all three men staring at her cute little bottom. Though he couldn't blame them, he made a mental note to remind them that they couldn't afford distractions. Jillie Everhart might be a definite hottie, but she was off-limits to all of them. Including him.

At the top of the stairs, she barely glanced to the right, where her bedroom was. Instead, she directed them to the other bedrooms, which were on the opposite side of the house.

"Gentlemen, take your pick." She spread her arms wide. "There are two guest bedrooms and four of you, so you'll have to double up."

Suppressing a yawn, she lifted her hand in a half-hearted wave. "Sorry to be a bad hostess, but I'm going to bed. I'll see y'all in the morning."

As she passed Seb, she reached out and gave his arm one final touch. "You don't get up too early, do you? I don't have to work tomorrow and I want to sleep in."

"Of course not," he lied, ignoring Ryan's raised brow. "Get some sleep."

"Thanks." She strolled off, turning one final time as she reached her doorway. "You all make yourselves at home. There's not much in the way of food, but you're welcome to whatever I have."

Seb nodded, noting that all three guys did the same. Not a single man spoke until Jillie closed her door with a decisive click.

"Daaaaaamn." Travis rubbed his eyes. "She looks even better in person than she does on TV."

"She's off-limits." Seb barked out the words. "No exceptions." He pointed to the first door. "Travis and Charlie, you sleep there. Ryan shares with me next door. Any questions?"

They shook their heads.

"Good." Seb strode off, knowing Ryan would follow.

Once they were alone in the room, Ryan dropped his bag on the floor and faced Seb. "Are you going to tell me?"

"Tell you what?"

Ryan looked Seb in the eye. "Exactly what's going on here?"

Seb stared straight back. "This is an assignment, nothing more."

"Commander, cut the bull. I've known you too long. You've changed. Is the woman the cause of that, or have the effects of whatever they did to you begun to wear off?"

"I wish." Seb crossed his arms. "Sometimes I think I can catch a glimmer of feeling, but it vanishes almost as soon as I become aware of it. Take this assignment. Knowing the bastards want me again should enrage me. But instead of angry, I feel…sharp and restless."

"That could be a plus, though. I'd rather be clear-headed than battling anger and frustration."

"A plus I've thought of, believe me," Seb said drily.

"See? That trace of irony in your voice. That's the old you. No offense, Seb, but you sounded like a robot every time we spoke."

"None taken." Rummaging in his duffel, Seb located his sleeping bag and shook it out.

After a moment's hesitation, Ryan did the same. "You haven't answered my question. What's going on between you and Jillie Everhart?"

"Not a thing." Briefly, Seb explained how he knew Jillie and what General Knight had told him. "I'm not sure how the media identified me from her blog, but that's what made the splinter cell think she'd make good bait to recapture me."

"And we played right into their hands. You're here to protect her, making you an easy target."

"That's the point. We're going to capture them. I want those bastards locked up. I want to know what they did to me and how to reverse it."

Ryan grinned. "There it is again—emotion. You sound furious. How can you say you still don't feel anything when plainly you do?"

Swallowing, Seb dragged his hand through his hair. "I don't know what's going on. And for right now, I can't allow myself the luxury of trying to figure things out. I've got to focus on this mission—on catching those SOBs."

"What agencies are involved besides the military?"

"The FBI counterterrorist unit is in charge. I'm sure the CIA is also involved on some level. I don't care, as long as the feebies stay out of my way."

Sliding in his sleeping bag, Seb turned his back to

the other man and closed his eyes. Hopefully, after a few hours sleep, he'd wake to find he had his equilibrium back.

Jillie's twin sister, Rachel, called at nine the next morning. Letting the cell phone ring, Jillie squinted at the caller ID with one bleary eye, saw Rachel's name, and snuggled back under her sheet. They could talk later, when she'd gotten enough sleep.

But Rachel was Rachel. The instant the call went to Jillie's voice mail, she hung up and redialed. She was perfectly capable of continuing to call until Jillie finally answered.

The ringing began to give Jillie a headache. Why prolong the agony?

With a groan, she reached for the phone. "Mmmph."

"Ah, you *are* awake." As usual, Rachel managed to sound both briskly efficient and loving.

"I am now. What do you want?"

Rachel gave a long, exaggerated sigh. "You know what I want. Spill. Seb's got to be there by now."

"He is. But keep it quiet. I don't want paparazzi camped outside my front door."

"They'll find out when you go back on tour, won't they? And I assume you aren't canceling any shows?"

Jillie couldn't help but smile at the worry in her sister's voice. Rachel had just been through a rough spot. She'd been accused of murdering her wealthy husband, and then threats were made against her and her son. The only bright spot during this time had been Seb's brother Dominic, Rachel's first love and, as it turned out, the love of her life. Jillie had never seen her twin so happy as she'd been since getting back together with Dom.

Now Rachel wanted the same thing for Jillie. Heck, Jillie wanted it, too.

"Seb wanted me to, but there's no way I can cancel this tour. The record label has put a huge amount of money into this album, and touring helps make records sell. Plus, I don't want to disappoint my fans."

"You'll disappoint them worse if you get captured by some crazed radical militants."

Jillie gave a rueful laugh. "That's what Seb said."

Rachel paused. When she spoke again, her voice was quieter, almost as if she wanted to make sure she wasn't overheard. "How's Seb? Any different?"

"Not really. Sometimes I think I can see a glimmer of something, but as soon as I look for it, it's gone."

"You sound sad."

With a sigh, Jillie pointed out the obvious. "Not sad, just tired. You did wake me up, you know."

Rachel ignored this. "Where is he now?"

"I have no idea." Stretching, Jillie stifled a yawn. "Probably still asleep."

"When he was here in Vegas, he was an early riser. The military trains them to be that way. He's probably been up for hours."

Jillie's pulse quickened at the thought of Seb, roaming around her house barefoot and shirtless.

"I guess I'd better go make coffee then. I hate to rush you off the phone." She paused for effect. "But if there's nothing else you have to tell me—"

"Call me later," Rachel said, rushing the words. She knew the drill.

"I will. Bye." As she hung up, the smoke alarms began to shriek.

Chapter 4

"Shoot." Seb dumped the still-smoking black lumps in the sink. "I forgot about the biscuits."

"You never could cook worth a damn." Ryan and Travis fanned a cookie sheet at the smoke detector, finally silencing its shrieking.

"And you probably woke up Jillie." Charlie sounded both eager and glum. "I hope she's not one of those women who's crabby when she gets woken up suddenly."

"She's not." Seb spoke without thinking, feeling his face heat up as they all turned to stare at him.

"How do you know?" Ryan arched his brow.

"Just a lucky guess." Forcing a laugh, Seb knew his explanation sounded weak. "I met her in Vegas and she was fine."

The coffeepot beeped to indicate it had finished brewing, saving him from explaining any further.

"At least you can make a decent pot of coffee." Ryan snagged a cup, filled it and passed it over to Seb.

"Thanks." Seb drank, ignoring the dig. "Since I burned the biscuits, there's no point in me trying to make the sausage and the gravy. Who wants to make a breakfast run?"

Travis and Charlie agreed to go. When they took off, Ryan and Seb were left alone in the kitchen.

"So?" Ryan grinned. "You gonna spill or what?"

"There's nothing to spill. Jillie's like family, a sister or something. Don't make more of it than it is."

"Riiight." Though Ryan's tone indicated his disbelief, he said nothing further. Instead, he took a long drink of coffee and watched Seb. "Why don't I believe you?"

"I don't care if you do or don't. Jillie really is like family to me."

"Family, huh?" Jillie stood in the doorway—her blue eyes still sleepy and golden hair rumpled.

Seb's stomach gave a peculiar lurch at the sight of her. Judging from the stunned expression on the other man's face, Ryan had a similar reaction. Seb couldn't blame him. Jillie looked both innocent and sexy as hell. And—he took a second look—furious. Evidently his words had royally pissed her off.

"Well, we *are* related in a way," he pointed out in his most reasonable tone.

She snorted. "Whatever." Flouncing into the kitchen, she flashed Ryan a brief smile and poured herself a cup of coffee. "What did you two do to make my smoke alarms go off?"

Ryan pointed to the sink and the charred biscuits. "The commander never could cook. If we'd known he was going to try to make something, we would have taken over."

Eyeing the black lumps decorating her sink, Jillie glanced from Ryan to Seb and then burst out laughing. The sound was so infectious that both men found themselves smiling.

"He said you were cheerful in the morning," Ryan pointed out, mischief in his tone. "I guess he was right."

This made Jillie laugh even harder, sloshing her coffee out on the floor. Not wanting her to burn herself, Seb grabbed her cup and placed it on the table while Ryan got a paper towel and wiped up the spill.

A moment later, Jillie grabbed a napkin, dabbed at her eyes and took a seat, still shaking her head. "I can see I'm going to have a lot of fun with you guys."

This time Ryan laughed, the sound of him full of masculine appreciation. If Seb felt a small burning in his belly, he knew it wasn't jealousy.

As sunlight slanted in through the window over the sink, they drank their coffee in companionable silence.

The other men soon returned with a bag of breakfast burritos and hash browns and set them on the table.

"I got one for you, too, Jillie," Charlie said, smiling self-consciously. "In case you were hungry."

"I am." Jillie grinned enthusiastically at him, making him blush. "Let me get some paper plates."

Once she'd finished setting the table with flowered

paper plates, matching napkins and plastic silverware, they all chowed down.

While eating, Seb eyed his men one at a time. Being back with his unit was good, and under normal circumstances, he knew he'd feel spectacular. What he thought he might feel instead was a vague sense of rightness, as if something within his shattered world had finally clicked in place. It wasn't true emotion—or at least he didn't think so—but for now, he'd take whatever he could get.

Once they'd finished and everyone had a chance to pour a second cup of coffee, they got down to business.

Seb began by outlining Jillie's touring schedule. "She's got a show in Dallas on Friday night, one in Houston on Saturday, and another in San Antonio on Sunday."

"Whew," Travis whistled. "That's a lot of traveling. How are we getting there?"

Before Seb could speak, Jillie answered. "Normally when I go on tour, I climb into the bus with the rest of my band and head out. The bus is like a superluxurious motor home and it's a lot of fun."

"But not this time?" Ryan guessed.

Jillie shook her head. "Nope. Unfortunately, my custom-made coach, which has every conceivable option, has my picture and name emblazoned on the sides. The FBI said the tour bus would be an easy target and General Knight agreed. Since I didn't want to endanger my band, I rented a second, unmarked bus for them."

"She insists on keeping everything as close to normal as possible," Seb said. "The regular bus went out, too, staffed by undercover FBI agents. The Feds have agents acting as her bodyguards. Other than that, it's up to us to keep her safe and catch these bastards."

When Seb mentioned the Feds, his men got identical expressions of disgust on their faces.

"Why are the Feebs involved?" Ryan asked. "They just get in the way."

"Not always." Knowing he had to foster an attitude of camaraderie and cooperation, Seb downplayed the news. "You guys know that my brother was an FBI negotiator for years. He did a lot of good. These guys might turn out to be a blessing in disguise." By some miracle, he managed to sound sincere. His acting ability had certainly developed since his imprisonment. He finished by saying, "Not all Feds are bad."

"Yeah, maybe not," Ryan agreed, though he didn't sound convinced. "But they sure can be a pain in the ass."

They all laughed. All of them except Jillie.

"What are we doing here?" she asked carefully.

"We're trying to work up a game plan," Travis noted. "Making sure you're protected and figuring out ways to dodge the Feds."

Seb nearly groaned out loud, guessing how she'd react to those words.

"Dodge the Feds?" Jillie frowned. "I thought we were all working together."

"We are." Seb tried to smooth things over. "Why don't you tell us what the routine is like when you're on tour?"

His distraction worked and Jillie provided them with the details.

"It's much less exciting than you would think," she began. "Usually it's a bunch of us packed into my tour bus. It's kind of fun, like a prolonged camping trip. But this time, not so much."

"When you say the bus has your name and picture on it—how big are we talking?" Charlie asked.

With a self-conscious smile, Jillie answered. "Giant pictures of me, on both sides. The record label suggested that. They said it'd be good advertising."

Both Charlie and Travis groaned out loud. Seb caught himself exchanging a grin with Ryan. Odd. He so rarely smiled anymore, yet ever since Jillie—

Projecting. He had to be projecting. Drumming up his fondest desire to become his former self and pathetically trying to make it reality.

This had to stop. He had a job to do, a bunch of creeps to catch. If he wanted to do it right, he couldn't let his emotional problems—or lack of them—get in the way.

"So what about you?" Travis asked. "How are you getting there?"

"You know," Jillie said casually, "I wanted to go with my band on the unmarked bus. That idea got shot down." She eyed Seb. "Same with using the record label's jet. When I asked General Knight what he wanted me to do, he told me to let Seb take care of my personal travel arrangements."

Seb nearly choked on his coffee.

"That's what I thought," Jillie said smoothly. "Since you haven't mentioned anything and General Knight didn't tell you when we met with him, I guessed you weren't told."

Grimly, Seb agreed. "I wasn't."

"Maybe it's not too late to book a couple of first-class tickets on a commercial airline."

"Absolutely not."

"Or," she continued as if he hadn't spoken, "we can hop in my Bentley and make the thirteen-hour drive to Dallas ourselves, though the other three guys would have to follow in their own vehicle."

For the first time since arriving in Boulder, Seb found himself at a loss for words.

"Either way, whatever is decided, we need to leave soon." Batting her long eyelashes at him, Jillie finished her coffee. Getting up, she went to the sink and rinsed out her cup.

"Let me know what you decide." Smiling at his guys, Jillie shot him an arched look over her shoulder as she left the room.

Driving into Texas was a bittersweet experience. Though Jillie had a Bentley, which would have been sweet to drive, Seb had elected to take her other vehicle, a nondescript Volvo SUV. In addition to having room for their gear, the Volvo wouldn't attract as much attention as the Bentley.

His men followed in their government-issued Jeep.

Driving through the arid plains of the panhandle was familiar. Though Seb hadn't taken this route in years, he had in the past. After all, his family lived in Dallas, though after his brother's wedding he'd worked hard to keep himself absent and out of their reach.

Being around them now was just too difficult. They watched him too closely, ready to jump on any evidence that he was getting better.

Though they'd asked why he was avoiding them, he couldn't give them that particular reason. It would hurt them needlessly. The closest he could come to an explanation was exhaustion. Plain and simple, he was bone tired—weary of trying to be the man he'd once been and aware that no one knew how to react to the man he'd become.

Watching Dom with Rachel—so happy, so in love—had been the final straw. He would never have even a tenth of what his brother had. No one loved someone who couldn't love them back.

Now, driving through the flat and dusty Texas plains with a woman who was more full of life than any woman he'd ever met, Seb wondered for the hundredth time if things would have been better all the way around if he'd been killed in that ambush rather than taken prisoner. He might as well be dead anyway. He knew his lack of emotion hurt his family and friends.

"'Welcome to Dalhart.'" Reading the sign, Jillie flashed him a wide smile, glancing around her excitedly, as if they'd just pulled into Hollywood or something. "Look at this place. I love it."

Seb looked around, trying to see what she saw. Squat brick buildings that looked as though they were wilting in the hot wind and fierce sun lined the four-lane road. In the distance, where the heat created a shimmery mirage on the horizon, grain elevators glinted in the sun. The town looked like a place built for endurance rather than enjoyment.

Downtown there were old-fashioned storefronts with front porches, wind chimes tinkling in the ever-present breeze and rocking chairs swaying from ghostly occupants. If not for the steady stream of cars, trucks, and recreational vehicles, the town might have stepped right out of the Wild West.

"Can we stop?" Eyes bright with excitement, Jillie practically bounced in her seat.

"Sure," Seb heard himself say, flicking on the signal and pulling into a parking spot in front of a lunch café. The Jeep pulled in a nearby spot.

Before Seb had even opened his own door, Jillie bounded out of the car. Instantly, Ryan, Travis and Charlie surrounded her.

"Hey," she protested, laughing. Her bright blue eyes locked on Seb's as he joined them. "Is this really necessary?"

"Yes." Though he hated to put a wet blanket over her enthusiasm, she needed to face the truth. "You're a high-profile person, Jillie. Aren't you used to having bodyguards nearby?"

"Yes, but not *this* many. And this is a public place. No one's going to try anything here, are they?"

All of his men kept identical, expressionless faces and let him handle the situation.

"They're *terrorists,* Jillie. *Terrorists.*" If his choice of words didn't make her realize what he meant, he didn't know what would.

Watching him, her wide smile slowly dimmed and the light in her beautiful eyes went out. Nodding carefully, she turned back toward the car, pushing at Ryan when he tried to block her.

"Let me go."

Ryan looked at Seb, waiting for permission.

"I'm going back to the car," Jillie said, her voice low and curiously flat. "Now let me go, please."

Seb jerked his chin, and Ryan stepped aside.

Avoiding his gaze, Jillie made her way to the car, opening the door and stepping inside without another word.

The guys all looked at Seb, who shrugged.

"Women," he muttered under his breath. "Looks like we're pulling out."

Once they'd got back on the highway, Jillie turned to him. He realized there were tears in her eyes. While he puzzled over this, she reached over and touched his arm. It was the lightest of touches, but still he had to suppress a shudder.

"What's wrong, Jillie?"

"I don't want you to get hurt." She waved her hand at the Jeep, four car lengths behind them. "Or them. This is ridiculous."

He waited for her to admit she was wrong, that she should have canceled her tour.

Instead, she sighed. "General Knight told me how important it is that I help catch these people, these…terrorists." She hesitated over the word, as though saying it was akin to cursing, which in a way it was.

"Catching them is not your job," he pointed out, as gently as he could. "You didn't ask for any of this."

Again she touched him and again he had to take care not to show how it unsettled him. "I posted about you on my blog. Thousands of people read what I said. The media picked it up and ran with it. My actions brought me to their attention."

Her smile, a flash of white between plump red lips, came and went. "I asked for it, Seb. Now, I want them caught as much as you do."

"I doubt that."

She stroked his arm. He told himself he didn't feel anything—and maybe he didn't emotionally—but his body reacted. Desire, never far from the surface when around Jillie, began a slow burn in his gut.

"Don't." One word, an order, his tone so harsh she withdrew her hand immediately.

"Sorry."

All the way into Wichita Falls, she was silent except for when she was humming along to the radio, which she'd put on a country music station.

Since he'd been back, Seb had avoided listening to music. He used to love all kinds, from heavy metal to rap to country. But music to him had always been about emotion. The beat of the drums, the whine and scream of the guitar, and the slow drawl of a singer's voice all spoke to the soul. Now he couldn't experience music properly. The purpose of a well-crafted song, the subtle pitch and range of a melodic voice, the honesty of a perfectly tuned guitar were completely lost on him.

He sensed the void his lack of reaction left in him. The experience was similar to when he'd see a spectacular sunset, or witnessed the sheer beauty of a horse running flat out to beat a storm, and still feel flat and empty. He'd lost much more than words could ever express.

Seb had never spoken of this to anyone. Most people took for granted everyday things—the nuances of a touch, the tear that came to one's eye when hearing a wonderful turn of phrase or catching sight of something spectacular.

Glancing at the vibrant woman beside him, he wondered. Humming to herself as she studied a map, Jillie lived for her music. And more. He remembered how she'd rushed to her sister's side when Rachel needed her and how she'd tried to take him under her wing, clowning around with him at first, then becoming serious—far too serious. As they'd spent time together and he'd gotten to know her, he'd seen more of her intensity.

When she decided on a course of action, she went all out, full throttle. As someone completely immersed in life, Jillie might just be one of the few people who could ever understand the immensity of Seb's loss.

Yet he couldn't tell her all that. To do so would invite a closeness he couldn't feel. He couldn't do that to her. She'd actually posted a blog stating she thought he was *The One,* and he'd never encouraged her or even responded to a single overture.

Nor would he.

"Is Wichita Falls about two and a half hours from Dallas?" Jillie asked, looking up from her map. At Seb's nod, she grimaced.

"Yes, so we're going to get there really early. I hate hanging around hotel rooms—they deplete my energy. I don't suppose you'd be willing to go the Galleria and be my bodyguard while I shop?"

He suppressed a smile at her hopeful expression. "Don't think so," he said lightly. "Maybe you can rehearse?"

"Rehearse?" She snorted, a sound that coming from her, somehow managed to sound completely feminine. "I've been on this tour for weeks now. I've got the act down cold. I don't need to rehearse. I need distraction."

Suddenly, he thought of his sister. Lea just might forgive all his transgressions if he brought her favorite country singer by the house. "My family is in Dallas," he said slowly. She'd met most of them at Dom's wedding. "Would you like to go see them?"

She lit up at his words, making him realize that under normal circumstances he'd feel guilty about letting her get her hopes up. To eliminate any misunderstanding, he clarified. "I just talked to my sister, Lea. She's one of your biggest fans."

Still smiling, Jillie nodded. "I remember her. Tiny little thing, but sweet as could be. Growing up must have been a challenge for her, especially with two big bruisers like you and Dom for older brothers."

"If you only knew." He glanced at her sideways. "That tiny little thing could probably kick my ass. She's a martial arts fanatic."

Jillie grinned. "I'd love to see her again. If you're sure you won't mind, let's stop and visit them."

"I don't mind." And the funny thing was, he didn't. If he could experience emotion, he might even say he was looking forward to it.

A couple hours later, they pulled up in front of the brick ranch house where Seb had grown up.

"Look at the trees," Jillie marveled. As soon as he put the shifter in Park, she sprang out of the car then waited impatiently for him to join her before practically bounding up the sidewalk.

Seb wished he had her energy. As usual, he pointed himself where he needed to go and, with no fuss, no liveliness, no emotion, went. Sometimes he wondered if he'd always been this way.

Ryan pulled up and parked behind Seb. Lifting his

hand to greet them, Seb continued to watch Jillie, telling himself it was only because he didn't dare take his eyes off his charge.

With the hot summer sun lighting up her golden hair, her worn denim shorts hugging her shapely thighs and showing off her long legs, she looked like the typical girl next door. Only she was ten times more beautiful than any girl next door he'd ever seen.

Behind him, Ryan made a startled sound, apparently agreeing with him.

Before Jillie even made it up the walk, the front door burst open.

"Jillie!" Lea shrieked, holding out her arms as though welcoming an old and much-missed friend.

"Lea!" Responding in kind, Jillie rushed to hug the petite, dark-haired woman.

Arms around each other's shoulders, chattering happily, the two women turned and went inside, completely forgetting him.

"Wow," Ryan said from behind him. While Seb had been intently watching the two women, his men had gotten out of the Jeep and joined him.

He had been too distracted to even notice. Seb swallowed hard. Distractions like that had a way of getting a man killed.

"Do you think she's always like that?" Wide-eyed, Charlie looked awestruck. Or Jillie-struck would be more accurate.

"Women are like that." Travis punched the younger man playfully. "Come on, bro. You're a marine. You can handle it."

Women weren't all like that, but Seb let the comment

go. Though he was barely ten years older than Travis, sometimes he felt like a lifetime separated them.

"Come on, let's go inside."

"Sounds good." Silently, they trailed Seb into his childhood home.

Here of all places, he would have thought he'd be overwhelmed with emotion. The memories were there. He could vividly recall his first day of school, kissing his first girlfriend—little Kimmie Carson—behind the giant banana tree, and his mom handing him one of a hundred or more fresh-baked chocolate chip cookies, the chocolate melting to a tiny puddle right in the middle.

But when he walked through the front door into the tiny foyer, he felt nothing.

The sound of Jillie's laughter, husky and sensual, reached him and the hair stood up on his arms.

"She's amazing," Charlie breathed.

"Off-limits," Seb barked. "I don't want to have to warn you again."

Ryan, Travis and Charlie all looked at him.

Had he gone too far? Hell, no, he decided instantly. Jillie was their charge. She didn't need hero worship or starstruck young kids making eyes at her. She needed them at their best—marine style.

Feeling a new purpose to his step, he strode into the kitchen, his men trailing after him, and stopped short at the sight of his mother. Her gray hair cropped short in a practical cut, her shoulders slightly rounded from the weight of her years, she beamed at him and his men before rushing over and enveloping him in a quick hug.

"Seb!" Joy rang in her voice. "How lovely! And you

brought friends, just like old times. I was just about to make dinner—how would you like my special fried chicken? You always love that, and I've added a few spices to the recipe, so I think—"

"Mom," Seb interrupted. "We can't stay. I brought Jillie to see Lea, but we have to go back downtown to get ready for her show."

"You brought Jillie?" If anything, her broad smile widened. "Where is she?"

"She's with Lea in the rec room. I'm sure they'll be in here in a minute or two. We're on a tight schedule."

Mrs. Cordasic blinked twice. "You still have to eat, don't you?" She glanced away from him toward his men, who stood watching. "I'll bet you boys would love some of my delicious fried chicken, wouldn't you?"

"Yes, ma'am." Charlie moved forward, eagerness shining from every pore. "It's been a long time since any of us had some home cooking."

The other men eyed him. They knew better than to speak. Orders were orders and Seb was in charge.

Seb vowed silently to have a word with Charlie. Although he'd spoken the truth, Charlie needed to be better disciplined. Seb cleared his throat in warning.

"Sorry, Commander," Charlie muttered. "I didn't think before I—"

"Nonsense," Mrs. Cordasic cut in, her voice sharp. "My son might be your boss, but you're all in my house now. If you have time to eat, you'll eat. Right, son?" Glaring at him, she dared him to contradict her.

The other men were stone-faced as they looked from Seb to his mother, but Seb swore he could see glints of desperate hope in all of their eyes.

He caved. "Let me go ask Jillie what time we have to be there, okay?"

Before he even finished the sentence, Lea and Jillie strolled into the room.

"Jillie!" Mrs. Cordasic greeted her enthusiastically, hugging her close while commenting on how long her hair had gotten.

Had it? Seb took another look. He really hadn't noticed any difference.

"I know it's early, but do y'all have time to eat?"

Jillie's grin encompassed them all. "Of course we do. As long as we can leave in an hour or two. Do you want me to go out and get something?"

"Of course not. I was going to make fried chicken, green beans and potatoes."

Jillie grinned. "My favorite. Let me help."

The women all began chattering. Seb took a step back, standing squarely with his men. Weird how, even in his own home, he felt like an outsider.

Chapter 5

Ninety minutes later, they were headed toward the American Airlines Center. While they were driving along Woodall Rogers, Seb watched for the sign for the Continental Avenue exit.

From the freeway, they could see the building. With four hours to go until the show, the concert venue was still deserted. Once they got inside the backstage area, however, chaos reigned.

Seb and his men, trailing on Jillie's heels, took care to appear as unobtrusive as possible. The Feds had people in the audience for extra security. Each of Seb's men took one corner of the stage, standing as much out of the way as they could. No one seemed to notice them. All eyes watched Jillie.

Jillie appeared to thrive on the chaos, prowling the

perimeters of the huge stage and greeting enthusiastically the men performing sound checks on the equipment. She vibrated energy.

Studying her, Seb *felt* energized, too. She flew around the stage—every movement animated—and looked blazingly, scorchingly alive. Even her beautiful eyes sparkled a more vivid, azure-blue.

Everyone around her appeared to react to her vibrancy.

"This is gonna be a good one tonight," she shouted, as another man tested out the drum kit.

"Hell, yeah." Someone answered from the shadows of the stage.

Equipment was tested, moved and tested again. Lights came on—white and red and yellow and blue—then went off in complicated patterns and setups. Band members straggled in, picked up their instruments, and performed their own tests. Jillie danced around them, bouncing from guitar to keyboard, laughing and singing. All the men grinned at her and high-fived her when she lifted her hand.

Seb wanted to feel what she did, even a tenth of that energy would be more than he had now.

Instead, he watched her whirl around the stage, aware that he was going to have to be extra protective of her once the crowds showed up. He'd made several attempts to get her to stop and listen to his plans, but she'd been too distracted to pay more than cursory attention.

After a few hours of this, finally, she appeared to be satisfied. Singing softly under her breath, she ran up to Seb and grabbed his arm.

"Come on. Everything's good here. Fans will start showing up soon. The gates open in a few minutes.

We've got to head back to my dressing room so I can get ready."

He nodded at her, then motioned to his men. Ryan went on ahead, Seb stayed at her side and Travis and Charlie brought up the rear.

They went down a narrow hallway. At a room marked with a gold star, Jillie stopped. "You guys will have to wait outside while I change."

Seb nodded. "That's fine, but I'm doing a sweep of the room first."

"Knock yourself out." Bouncing up on the balls of her feet, she stepped aside.

A quick inspection revealed a small but luxurious room. The thermostat had evidently been set to ensure the air conditioning blew full blast.

"All clear," Seb told her, exiting the room. "I should warn you, it's freezing in there."

"I like it that way." Still glowing, she beamed up at him.

He had the fiercest impulse to kiss her. Knowing his men stood directly behind him was the only thing that kept him from acting on it.

"Wait here." She turned to go inside, then suddenly spun. Standing up on tiptoe, she placed a quick kiss on his cheek. "Thank you," she said, then stepped away, closing the door firmly between them.

"Whew." Ryan whistled. "Lucky you."

Seb frowned then shook his head like a dog shaking off a blow. "No," he muttered. "I wish she'd stop doing that."

Charlie's laugh trailed off when he saw Travis and Ryan's hard looks. Seb didn't even bother looking at him. Charlie made him feel old. Old and tired.

Five minutes later, the hairstylist and the makeup artist, both women, arrived. Seb verified their credentials and they disappeared inside with Jillie. Finally the dressing room door opened and Jillie blew through it. The red silk evening dress looked as though it had been poured on to her.

They all stared. Seb cleared his throat, delivering a warning to them.

Jillie didn't appear to notice. She only had eyes for Seb.

"I'm ready," she said brightly. Her vibrancy electrified the room. "I just got the call. Five minutes until curtain. They'll be announcing me, so we've got to get back to the stage." Her laugh, though nervous, rippled through the air, infectious and infused with life.

Watching her, Seb realized this woman was everything he was not—everything he'd never be. Once again he launched into the instructions of what to do in the event they had to evacuate. She nodded in all the right places.

When he finished, she pressed a hand to his cheek then brushed past him and seemed to float down the hall.

His men, marines to the soul, simply stared. Seb barked out orders then hurried to catch up to her, Ryan at his heels.

"And now...the very beautiful, very talented, Jillie Everhart!" The announcer's voice boomed over the loudspeakers.

Jillie bent her bead, muttered something under her breath—perhaps a quick prayer—and blazed forth.

Seb and Ryan positioned themselves, one on each side of the stage, as Jillie launched into a rousing country song that sounded vaguely familiar, though Seb didn't know the words.

Though his focus remained on the crowd, every so often his gaze fell on Jillie. As he watched her prance and sing and cajole the audience, he marveled. So many facets. So much soul, with such a bright light. No wonder she'd made it big.

She was amazing—a Superstar with a capital *S*. He should be honored to guard her and not feel so conflicted.

Jillie sang, strutting around the stage as if she owned it. And she did. She gave her everything to the performance. Every song was special to someone and every listener had their personal favorites.

The crowd got on their feet for the fast-paced, bootscootin' stuff and were quietly pensive for the heart-rending ballads. At one point, Jillie herself even broke down in tears as she sang about the sacrifices soldiers make for regular people. She privately dedicated that particular tune to Seb.

Although he didn't know it, throughout the entire concert she was achingly, thrilling conscious of him standing off to the edge of the stage. His presence gave her a little extra boost, not that she needed one. By the time she reached the next to last song, she knew she'd given one of her best concerts ever.

Performing was her own particular high. She didn't need alcohol or drugs. Just this—the pouring of herself into every note and the sea of bright, expectant faces bathed in the white lights as the spotlights searched the crowd.

When she sang, power rippled through her out into the cosmos, into the crowd, where it grew and swelled and traveled right back. Often she felt like a vampire of sorts, feeding off the energy from the fans, drinking it in, and pouring it back out in her notes, in her sweat.

This was what she had been born to do. Her life was complete and sinfully happy. She had everything she needed. She'd never thought she'd want anything else.

Until she'd taken one look at Seb's chiseled face and begun to realize there might be something more.

She glanced at him, still standing to the side of the stage, waiting in the shadows, and she let the thought go. Her desires were too complicated.

Bowing, she finished the set and the show. As the clapping started, she danced off stage, knowing that although the lights had gone out, she wasn't done. The thundering applause grew louder, taking on a rhythm, keeping perfect beat to the crowds chanting.

They wanted more, as they always did.

After a quick nod at her bandmates, they ran back on stage, waiting for her and starting up the beat of one of her most popular hits.

The crowd went wild as Jillie danced out, singing joyously, her voice barely tired. She couldn't see Seb, couldn't feel him, and though this fleetingly worried her, her energy had begun to flag and she had to let go and focus on the song and her fans.

Then, too soon, the show was over. She was done.

She didn't see Seb or his men as she rushed past the stage hands, but she had no doubt they were close on her heels. She'd promised not to go anywhere without Seb by her side, but with her emotions so high she couldn't seem to stop her forward momentum.

Jillie's main focus was on getting back to her dressing

room, so she could close the door and feel the surge of joy that came from knowing Seb had shared this experience with her. She counted herself truly lucky and blessed.

She glanced over her shoulder, saw Seb moving rapidly toward her, running to reach her side. His intent focus made her feel cherished, protected, safe.

Flashing him a grin, she resumed her forward progress, knowing he would have her back.

As she bounded along the corridor, a man came out of nowhere and grabbed her, his face in shadows. She reacted instantly, the way she'd been taught to do in the self-defense class she'd taken.

Pivot and thrust. Elbow in the ribs, a twist, one sharp kick and he released her with a grunt.

Jillie lifted her dress, kicked off the heels that would only hamper her and took off running.

She kept going, gasping for air as she heard his footsteps pounding right behind her.

"Seb," she screamed, wanting him. She risked a look back and saw him gaining on her attacker, Ryan not far behind him.

Her pursuer drew closer, grabbing her by the hair and spinning her around with a painful jerk. She screamed again.

Then Seb was there, yanking the guy off her. He punched him hard, and the assailant went down.

Seb grabbed her, pushing her out of the way and against the wall, blocking her with his body. The other men appeared, rounding the corner at the end of the hall at a dead run.

Springing to his feet, the attacker took off.

"Ryan, Charlie, after him," Seb roared. He pointed to Travis. "You, back to your post. I'm staying with her."

Ryan and Charlie raced by Jillie, passing her just as the attacker reached the door to the stairwell at the far end of the hall. Travis had vanished, evidently returning to her dressing room.

Still stunned, Jillie took a deep breath. Glancing down at her hands, she realized she was shaking.

"Can you believe that?" She turned to Seb, adrenaline and emotion roaring through her. Grabbing his shirt, she asked, "How did that man get in here?"

Seb narrowed his eyes. "I don't know. We had security beefed up. Everyone—food vendors, ushers, cleaning people—had to be cleared. You can be sure we'll get answers."

He made no attempt to remove her hands and free himself. She searched his face, looking for regret, fear, worry—something. Anything.

But as usual, his handsome face looked perfectly blank.

Suddenly, she wanted to hurt him, yank him up against her, and make him *feel*. Something. She wanted him to show some expression, anger, disgust, anything but this complete and utter blankness.

"You're supposed to protect me!" She tightened her grip on his shirt, fisting the material in her hands. "How could this happen?"

As her voice rose, she saw the other men were returning. Ryan and Charlie jogged toward them, empty-handed. Travis emerged from her dressing room.

"He got away," Ryan said. "Don't know where he went. We split up to look for him, but he could be anywhere. There are thousands of workers here. All he had to do was grab a uniform and blend in."

Charlie looked at Jillie. "I'm sorry. Security is searching for him."

She couldn't be nice, not now. Her entire body shook as if she'd fallen into icy water. "This better not happen again, do you hear me?"

Seb and Ryan said nothing, though Seb raised his brow as if he knew that the seriousness of the threat had finally reached her. Charlie's freckled face colored as he looked down at his feet.

She realized she still had hold of Seb's shirt. Just as she started to release him, he caught her hands, holding them in his.

Seb stared at Jillie. "Travis, check the doorway. He has to be hiding somewhere. Charlie, secure the dressing room. Ryan, follow his trail as far as you can again, and see if there's a hidden exit."

"Commander—?" Ryan started, closing his mouth as Seb shot him a warning glare. "Never mind."

Once Charlie cleared the room, Seb herded Jillie inside. "Close the door and stand guard."

Once the door clicked shut, Seb let her go.

Jillie turned her back to him because she found his stone-faced expression unbearable.

"I can understand why you're angry," he said.

She didn't turn around. "Can you? I doubt that."

"The threat just became real to you, didn't it? I'm sorry."

Every word he spoke in that deep, masculine monotone added kindling to the fire of her anger and made her shake even more. She didn't know whether it was from rage or adrenaline. All she knew was that she hated feeling so weak, so exposed.

"Damn it, Seb, this was one of the best shows I've ever done. I wanted to celebrate. With you. Now, I want to punch something."

"Punch me."

Struck dumb, she finally turned to stare at him. "Are you freaking serious?"

Slowly, he nodded, making her realize once again that he really didn't care either way what she did. Seb was a gorgeous and sexy man, but he might have been a robot for all he felt. Punching him would make her feel worse, not better.

"No, I'm not punching you." She sighed, willing her trembling to stop. "The hotel has a workout room. I'll ask them to close it off for an hour and I'll swat at the punching bag."

He nodded, his hard gaze still holding hers. "I can promise you this. I *will* find out where the breech in security occurred."

"Can you promise it won't happen again?"

"In a contained environment," he began, breaking off when she frowned. "The Feds are handling a lot and we're coordinating with them, but unless we bring out the National Guard, shut down the concession stands, and vet the identification of every single concert goer, there's no way." His voice softened. "You were good tonight."

"Good?" Making a face, she scowled at him. "Are you trying to distract me?"

"Talk off the jitters. It helps, believe me."

She sighed. "Fine. But good is such a bland little word."

"You're right. You were better than good. You were phenomenal."

"Phenomenal? Sounds like an I-screwed-up-so-I'd-better-suck-up compliment." When he started to speak, she held up her hand. "Seb, I'm not after compliments. You don't have to do that. As a matter of fact, I'd prefer you didn't."

Crossing his arms, he glared at her. "I'm not doing anything. This might have been my first country music concert, but I really thought you were good."

"Your first country concert? You've been to other concerts though, right? I'm guessing rock, maybe heavy metal?"

He nodded. "I went to a few rock concerts as a teenager, but I've never been a country music fan. I had no idea."

There was something in his voice. Slowly, she moved closer, willing him to look at her, her breath catching in her throat, her heart pounding. Had that been appreciation she'd heard?

When he finally met her gaze, she realized it had been a false hope because he looked no different than he always did.

In that instant, more than anything, she wanted his expression to change.

"Seb?"

He cocked his head, waiting patiently, a perfect soldier robot, unfeeling.

That was the last straw.

Though she knew he understood intellectually how much danger she'd been in tonight, she wanted him to *feel*. Even just a little bit.

So Jillie, with adrenaline still simmering in her blood, did what she'd been wanting to do ever since she'd first laid eyes on him.

She grabbed him and then kissed him. Certain and sure, she slanted her mouth over his, willing him to react.

After a moment, he did.

Low in his throat, he made a sound, pulling her up against him and taking control of the kiss. He tasted her, branded her, made love to her with his tongue.

She'd wanted more.

She'd wanted a reaction and she got one. His breathing quickened and she could feel the force of his arousal pressing against her belly.

Whatever had been done to him evidently had no impact on that part of his physique.

When she finally broke the kiss, they both were breathing heavily. Gazing at him, noting the desire clouding his eyes, she wished for more than a physical reaction, but the one thing she wanted—emotion—was the very thing he was not capable of giving.

When he touched her shoulder, she jumped.

"Don't try to make me into something I'm not, Jillie. I can't be the man you need, at least not now. Maybe not ever."

She nodded. "I still want you," she whispered. "I don't know why, but I do."

To her chagrin, he chucked her under the chin. "I still want you, too, but some things just aren't meant to be. Come on, you need to get changed. I'll wait outside the door."

"Then what?" She crossed her arms. "If I have to sit around worrying about this, I'll go crazy. I need a distraction."

"We can go out and I can show you Dallas, if you like."

As she stared up at him, exhaustion hit her, hard enough to buckle her knees. She shook it off. "Just you and me?"

"From the car," he clarified. "It would be too dangerous to go inside any bars or clubs."

"No dancing?"

He shook his head.

She tried something else. "How about we rent a movie and watch it in my room, just the two of us?"

"You watch. I'll guard your door."

Of course. Jillie sighed.

More than anything, she wanted a distraction. But she wanted the kind Seb wasn't willing to provide, the kind involving sweaty bodies and tangled sheets.

They had another show tomorrow, plus a four-hour drive to Houston. Besides, she needed to go somewhere private and lick her wounds.

"I need to rest. TV will be fine for tonight," she lied.

Seb went to the door and opened it. Giving her a long, hard look, he nodded. "I'll be right outside the door. Are you going to be all right?"

"Of course." Pasting a smile on her face, she spoke with a lightness she didn't really feel. The adrenaline rush had faded and exhaustion had fully set in.

Her stomach growled, and she thought of a Mexican

place where she'd eaten last time she was in Dallas. Well, maybe TV wasn't the only option tonight after all.

Once he'd closed the door to Jillie's dressing room, Seb took a deep breath, then another. Since his return stateside, he'd had sex a few times. Meaningless, no-strings-attached sex. The only kind he was capable of now.

His men waited at the other end of the hallway.

Grateful his massive erection had subsided Seb motioned Ryan over.

Ryan held up a cell phone. "Charlie was able to snap some pictures of that guy. They're blurry, but we sent them to Sierra. She's already come back with a match."

Sierra was the Shadow Unit's very own computer genius and Intel expert.

"And?"

"He's on the list not to be allowed into the country."

"How'd he get in?"

"I assume a lax border inspection. Anything else?"

"He works for the same group that captured you." Ryan closed the cell phone with a snap. "The police nabbed him for speeding about twenty minutes ago. He was taken to a police station in Irving, right off the main boulevard."

"I know the place." Seb rubbed his hands together. "Things are finally looking up. I can't wait to talk to the bastard."

Ryan swallowed, looking uncomfortable. "Umm, you can't. He's already been picked up."

"Picked up?" Seb stared. "No way any government agency moved that fast."

"You know the Feds do, especially when national security is involved."

The curse Seb let loose would have made a sailor blanch, but Ryan didn't even flinch.

"I suppose they won't let us question him."

"That's right. General Knight just called a minute ago. He says our orders are to stay with Jillie. He wants the feebs to handle the interrogation."

"He called you?" As commander, Seb should have been the one to get the call.

"Yeah. Maybe you should check your phone. The general said he tried you first, but you didn't answer."

Seb reached in his pocket for his cell. He encountered nothing.

"It's gone." Immediately, he started searching the floor in the hall. "I bet it fell out when I was fighting that guy."

"Fan out," Ryan told the others. "Look."

They searched the hallway but found nothing.

Refusing to leave his post at Jillie's door, Seb watched them.

As they headed back toward him, Ryan's cell phone rang.

He held it up. "It's your number calling," he told Seb.

"Let me have it." Snatching the phone, Seb flipped it open. "Hello."

"Next time, you won't get away so easily," a heavily accented voice said. "You have a choice. Give yourself up or we will kill the woman." The man hung up.

Slowly, Seb stared at the phone. His path seemed clear—he knew what he had to do, and quickly.

Using Ryan's speed dial, he scrolled until he found

the direct line to General Knight and punched Send. The general picked up on the third ring.

"I want off this case," Seb said. His chest hurt so badly he could barely get out the words.

Silence. General Knight's lack of immediate response was no doubt due to shock that Seb would actually call to try and decline an assignment.

"What are you talking about?" the general barked. "So far everything appears to be going according to plan. We're getting closer and closer to catching the SOBs."

"Jillie's going to get hurt."

"Son, you're a soldier. Do your job and protect her. Hell, even the president has a special interest in that woman. She's an international celebrity. It wouldn't look good for our country's defense if we can't even protect one little country music singer."

As Seb opened his mouth, he heard a decisive click as General Knight hung up the phone.

"What if I can't protect her?" he asked under his breath, knowing nothing but dead air heard him.

Snapping the phone closed, he didn't even bother to curse. How could he, when he didn't even know who the hell he was anymore? He didn't like it one bit that he didn't recognize the man he'd become. If he wasn't comfortable in his own skin, he wouldn't be at his best to do what he had to do. Save Jillie. Capture the SOBs who'd changed him.

And maybe, finally, find some frigging peace.

Chapter 6

Forcing herself to move, Jillie changed into regular clothes. She washed off the heavy stage makeup, replacing it with a light dusting of powder, and brushed out her hair. All that hairspray made her feel uncomfortable.

She didn't want to face Seb and his team until she felt more herself. She couldn't shake the lethargy that practically immobilized her. She stared in the dressing room mirror, willing herself to get up.

Hearing their voices in the hall outside her dressing room, Jillie started. She took a deep, calming breath, knowing Seb would still be guarding her, and took a final look in the mirror. Her attempt at a disguise included pulling her long hair back in a ponytail, donning a baseball cap, and wearing huge sunglasses. She'd tried it in Vegas and done okay, but it wouldn't fool people for long.

After checking her hands to see how badly she was shaking, she opened the door.

Ryan, Travis, Charlie and Seb stood in a huddle in the hall. They all glanced at her when she peered out. Though her gaze drifted over them all, she immediately focused on Seb.

Though he attempted a nonchalant smile, the fury she saw in his face stunned her. While she gaped at him, he seemed to realize something was amiss. In the next instant, all emotion vanished from his expression and normal, unflappable Seb returned. But this time, she knew she hadn't imagined what she'd seen.

Moving carefully, she closed the distance between them.

"What's wrong?" she asked softly, keeping her gaze on him, wishing she had the nerve to wrap her arms around him and hold on for dear life. She suspected they'd both feel better if she could.

"Wrong?" He shook his head, handing a cell phone back to Ryan before returning his gaze to meet hers. "They just called. They've got my phone, and they used my stored numbers to call Ryan."

She stared at him. "They called you?"

"Yeah." Swallowing, he kept his full attention on her. "Jillie, it's apparent that they aren't playing games. I tried to tell General Knight civilians have no business—"

She cut him off. "What did they say?"

Glaring at her, he swallowed again. "They threatened to kill you unless I turn myself in."

Though his words shocked her, she managed a nonchalant shrug. "So? Isn't that what they've been saying all along?"

All three men exchanged looks.

"No," Seb said. "They were going to capture you and use you as bait to lure me to them."

"That's right." Now she remembered. "But now, since they've learned you're right here at my side, they decided to take a shortcut?"

He jerked his head in something that resembled a nod. "Exactly."

"From what little I've heard about what happens in their prisons, I'd rather be dead."

Her words surprised him. She could tell even though his facial expression never changed.

"You're still not taking this seriously enough," Seb began.

Charlie interrupted. "Jillie, these guys don't care about anything but their goal. They'll kill you without batting an eye."

Seb shot a cool glare at his man. "They don't care how many other people get hurt—your band, your roadies, your fans."

Her legs suddenly felt weak. "I hadn't thought of that."

Charlie touched her arm, earning another hard look from Seb. "Of course you hadn't. How could you? You don't think like them."

Through all this, Seb had remained impassive, his muscular arms crossed. "Jillie, I won't push anymore tonight, but you need to rethink this tour thing."

"I'll sleep on it," she promised. "Now, I'd like to get something to eat. I burn a lot of energy when I perform."

Seb frowned. "I've already told you, we can't go to a crowded restaurant. Not now. Why don't I have one of the guys get something? We can eat in your room."

"That's exactly what they'll expect," Jillie argued. "Look, I'm not asking for too much. A quick meal, in and out. I've been planning to go to this place ever since I learned I'd be doing a show in Dallas. All I want is a margarita, some chips and hot sauce and chicken fajitas. With all four of you surrounding me, plus this disguise, I should be just as safe."

Seb's men watched them, waiting to hear his decision.

"Fine." Finally, he relented, his grim expression making it plain he wasn't happy about doing so. "But you don't get out of the car until I say so, and you walk in the middle of all of us. Agreed?"

She nodded.

Seb took them to the local Mexican restaurant she mentioned. Even at this late hour, the place was crowded. Seb parked the car and they got out, waiting for the guys to find a spot for their Jeep.

"It's nearly midnight and this place is still packed," Charlie said. "Must be popular."

"They have live bands until one." Seb opened the door, stepping aside to allow Jillie to precede him. "Not to mention that their fajitas are the best in town."

Inside the packed dining room, they had to shout to be heard over the noise. A few minutes after placing her order, Jillie excused herself, claiming she needed to use the ladies' room.

As she'd known he would, Seb followed her.

"I can get in trouble for this, but I have to check out

the inside," he told her, leaning close to her ear so she could hear him. "If someone's in there, I want you to wait until the restroom is empty."

A shiver went through her at the feel of his breath against her ear, but she simply nodded. He peeked in the door, then pushed it open wide. As luck would have it, the restroom was empty.

"I'll just be a minute." As soon as the door closed behind her, she took out her cell phone and punched in the code to speed dial her manager, Ron. Her call would probably wake him, but if she was going to cancel concerts, she needed him to start working on getting the word out as quickly as possible.

When he answered, she quickly filled him in on what happened and outlined her plan. "I'll do the Houston show tomorrow, but cancel San Antonio and the other shows."

"Are you sure about this?" Though sleepy, Ron sounded disgruntled. "Every concert is a sellout. As you know, we scheduled second shows in some of the larger cities. Canceling will cost you—and your sponsors—a truckload of money. Worse, it might hurt your reputation as an artist. Are you one hundred percent certain?"

"Positive," she said firmly. "No way do I want anyone injured or killed because of me. I'll call Marty in the morning and have him put a positive spin on things." Marty was her PR guy. "Everything will be fine, you'll see."

"Why not call Marty now? You had no problem waking me up. Why's he special?"

"He's grouchier than you are." Jillie summoned up

a lighthearted laugh. "Keep me posted on your progress, okay?"

Grumbling under his breath, Ron finally agreed to
do what he could, as long as she let him go back to sleep.

Finally, she emerged from the washroom to find Seb
blocking the door. Two other women, apparently highly
irritated at being denied access, stood next to him.

Spying Jillie, one shot her a furious look. The other,
younger, tan and blond, fluttered her eyelashes at Seb.
"Can we go in now?"

The hand gesture he used was the same one he
employed to swat away mosquitoes.

The women left in a huff, disappearing into the
ladies' room.

"Are you all right?" he asked, putting his hand on her
shoulder in a possessive way.

If he knew her better, he'd recognize that the brilliant smile she gave him was utterly fake. "Just fine," she
said. "I smell fajitas and I'm starving. Let's go eat."

The fajitas had arrived, and the second Seb and
Jillie appeared, the others dug in. She'd never had
such tasty Mexican food, and ate far more than she
normally did.

"You sure can put away tortillas," Charlie teased.
Even Ryan and Travis smiled at his comment, though
Seb's expression never changed.

"I work it off," she teased back, grabbing her last
flour tortilla and rolling up the rest of her chicken
inside. She took a huge bite with all of them watching
and rolled her eyes at Charlie.

Later, after they'd eaten and Seb had taken her back
to her hotel, she stood at the door to her room and

wondered if she dared stand on tiptoe and kiss him good-night.

"I'm not going anywhere," he told her. "I promise."

"I know, but—" she eyed the king-size bed. She'd never sleep if they had to share. Temptation would keep her awake all night.

He shook his head as if he'd read her thoughts and didn't approve. "No worries. Your suite has a hide-a-bed in the couch. I checked. When my shift is up, I'll sleep there."

Knowing she had no choice, Jillie stepped aside, allowing him into her room. Once he'd entered, she closed the door, locked the deadbolt and attached the chain.

As she got ready for bed in the bathroom, Jillie couldn't rid herself of the sense of excitement, the quiver of anticipation she felt low in her belly. She dressed for the night as she always did—in a pair of sleep shorts and a ribbed tank top.

A few moments later, she emerged from the bathroom with her face scrubbed clean. Feeling unusually self-conscious, she crossed her arms to cover her chest as she made her way across the room to the bed.

Though she tried to pretend he wasn't there, she felt Seb's gaze like a brand and instinctively glanced over. A mistake. Seb had stripped down to a pair of boxer shorts. His muscular chest was a sight to see.

He rose in one fluid motion and she sucked in her breath. Heavens, he was beautiful. She stood frozen at the edge of her bed, watching in awe and lust as he passed her, holding her breath until he'd gotten halfway across the room.

Then she noticed the scars. They crisscrossed his back, side-to-side. He looked like he'd been filleted.

She must have gasped or made some sound because he turned, one brow raised in question. "Something wrong?"

Silently, she shook her head. Swallowing, she looked away.

"Jillie?"

Slowly, she looked back at him.

"Does it repulse you?"

Though he had no way of showing it, the vulnerability shown by his question brought tears to her eyes.

She moved closer, stopping when he took a step back.

"They did that to you?"

"Yes. It took several surgeries to repair the cut muscles. And I have so much metal inside me, I set off metal detectors." His attempt at a wry smile hurt her heart. "The good thing about it is that most of it didn't hurt. Just the ones on my head. I don't even remember them doing a lot of it."

Clearing her throat, she tried to continue the conversation as though she wasn't affected. "How is that possible?"

"Drugs, I'm guessing. They kept me mostly unconscious for a couple of months. They'd revive me to test whatever new thing they'd done, then knock me out again."

Never one to pretend, Jillie couldn't contain her shock. "Months?"

"Yeah." Another failed attempt at a smile. "I guess I'm lucky my guys rescued me, but there ain't a woman in the world who's gonna want me now, which is probably all for the best, right?" Without waiting for an answer, he turned and closed the bathroom door behind him.

Jillie was completely blown away. A back full of scars couldn't make her—or any woman—not want him. Just watching the man made her ache with need.

When she'd left Vegas after meeting him, she'd dated other guys, but no man could begin to measure up. She hadn't even been able to bring herself to kiss any of them good-night.

She wanted to do much more than kiss Seb.

Seeing Seb the first time had brought a rush of physical attraction, a red-hot bolt of lust. Watching him help his brother and her sister, she'd recognized a good man—the rock-solid kind one could depend on. The dedication of his men had further bolstered her belief in him.

One week, and she'd been in love.

Closing her eyes, she suddenly, fiercely wished she had a sexy negligee and a couple of shots worth of courage. Of course, she had to smile at the thought. She had no idea how to seduce someone, wouldn't know the right way if she tried.

Shaking her head at her own foolishness, Jillie slipped beneath the sheets, plumped her pillow and closed her eyes. Since they had to get an early start, she knew she needed to get some rest, though how much sleep she'd get with Seb so close, she didn't know.

Seb's body was throbbing as he went through the motions of preparing for bed and tried to rationalize what had just happened.

Nothing. Absolutely nothing had happened. Why, then, had his body gone rock hard at the sight of Jillie in her casual nightclothes?

He splashed cold water on his face and debated taking a quick, cold shower, but decided against it. All he had to do was walk past her bed to his couch bed.

When he exited the bathroom, he realized she'd fallen asleep.

Stopping by the side of her plush bed, staring down at her, he felt an unfamiliar tightness in his chest. It might have been the spicy Mexican food, but somehow Seb sensed the ache was tied up with wanting Jillie.

Shaking his head at his own stupidity, Seb went to the sofa bed and tried to get some sleep.

Jillie's cell phone rang at 8:00 a.m. sharp. Seb's body ached as he listened to her sleepy voice say hello. He'd spent the night mostly awake, burning with desire for her. Now he not only had a four-hour drive but a four-hour drive alone with her in the car.

Hopefully, he wouldn't spend the entire drive aroused, though he suspected he might have to.

"Yes, Marty, I'm canceling. I've already talked to Ron." The sleepy tone quickly vanished from her voice. "I've no doubt you can put a positive spin on this. After all, that's what you do, right?"

There was a moment of silence while she apparently listened to whoever was on the other end.

Seb sat up, dragging his hand through his hair. She'd canceled her shows? When?

When she finished her call, she smiled at him. "I

guess you overheard. That was Marty, my public relations man. I talked to Ron, my manager, last night. I'm still doing Houston tonight, but everything else has been postponed."

"I'm glad," he said simply. "That was the right thing to do."

Her smile took his breath away.

"I guess." Jumping up from her bed, she made a mad dash for the bathroom. "Dibs on first shower," she sang out, sticking her tongue out at him right before closing the door.

He sat for a moment, frozen in the grips of intense lust, then took a deep breath. Trying not to picture Jillie naked in the shower, Seb called Ryan. The other man answered on the first ring, sounding as though he'd been awake for hours.

When Seb told him the news, Ryan cheered quietly. "This will make protecting her much easier. I'll tell the others."

Eyeing the still-closed bathroom door, Seb forced his thoughts back to the call. "Send Travis to guard our door while I shower, and let's all meet in the lobby in an hour. We need to get on the road. We can get breakfast at some drive-through."

After hanging up the phone, Seb turned on the TV, checked the weather, and clicked it off. A few minutes later, Jillie bounded from the bathroom, still toweling her long hair.

"Your turn!"

Unable to speak, Seb looked outside the door and gave Travis a nod, then strode to the bathroom. It looked like he needed to take another cool shower this morning, which made him wonder if he'd ever take a hot shower again.

By the time he emerged from the bathroom, Jillie had tucked her damp hair into a ponytail, donned a baseball cap and packed.

"You get ready quicker than any woman I've ever seen." Seb gave her the compliment truthfully.

"Lots of practice," she quipped.

They joined Travis and rode down the elevator in companionable silence. He appreciated how Jillie, unlike many other women, didn't feel a compulsive need to chatter.

As soon as the elevator doors opened on the lobby floor, Seb knew they were in trouble. Crowds of people milled around in the seating area, and the instant they saw Jillie, they rushed over. Flashbulbs went off, a storm of them. Microphones were thrust at them, reporters asking question after question, each attempting to talk over the others.

Instinctively, Seb and Travis went into defensive mode. Ryan and Charlie, exiting from the elevator next to them, rushed over and the men formed a protective half circle.

Where the hell were the Feds? They'd insisted they'd have the lobby secured.

"Sebastian Cordasic," someone shouted.

Hearing his name, Seb winced. The Cordasic family preferred to do their work as anonymously as possible.

For some reason, his name seemed to cause almost as much excitement as Jillie's.

Microphones were thrust at him, the babble of voices nearly unintelligible.

"...he's The One."

"...night together in this hotel..."

More flashbulbs, more shouts, people pushing, shoving, yelling.

"Enough!" Seb yelled, momentarily quieting the babble of voices. "Fall back," he told his men.

With one fluid motion, they all stepped back inside the elevator. Ryan punched the button and the doors closed.

"Now what?" Jillie appeared amused by the entire thing. At Seb's questioning look, her smile widened. "This kind of craziness is normal for me. I guess I'm used to being a celebrity."

Celebrity. He'd started to see Jillie as a person—a woman—and forgot that when she wasn't performing she was still a famous individual, someone who craved the limelight.

Seb's nature and the type of career he'd chosen ensured he avoided the limelight as much as possible.

Until now.

He thought of his grandfather, Phillip, bedridden and ill, but with a mind as sharp as a tack. The elderly man would definitely have something to say if he happened to see Seb on television.

And it wouldn't be nice.

"Someone's head is gonna roll," he growled. "The Feds assured me they'd secured the hotel."

"Where are they anyway?" Ryan crossed his arms. "They seem to be conspicuously absent. Did General Knight pull some strings to keep them in the background?"

"I don't know," Seb answered. "But I plan to find out."

"What do you normally do in a situation like this?" Charlie asked Jillie. "How do you leave the hotel?"

"Usually, I talk to one of the maids. They love to help. The hotel employees have their own elevators and know different routes in and out of the building. I take them and the paparazzi don't see me leave."

"How did they find out you were staying here?" Seb had taken care to ensure they hadn't been followed after they left the restaurant the night before.

Her bright blue gaze met his. "Honestly, this is probably the doings of my PR guy Marty. Remember I called him earlier? His job is to generate as much excitement about me as possible."

"Not good for security," Ryan muttered.

"My entire occupation isn't good for the type of security you have in mind."

Seb refused to be distracted. "Even if the mob of reporters is due to your public relations man, I didn't hear you tell him anything about where you were."

"I didn't have to. He knows my schedule." Then she explained how Marty had stepped up the hype about her and Seb to sell out more concerts.

Seb stared at her. "And you're okay with this?"

A smile played around her full lips, and she nodded. "It was before the terrorist thing happened. I pay Marty big bucks to handle my public relations. He knows what he's doing. I trust him."

"But the paparazzi—" Charlie began.

"The paparazzi are harmless. They're just doing their job, just like everyone else."

Seb couldn't resist pointing out what seemed obvious to him and his men. "Terrorists could disguise themselves as photographers. This would give them both anonymity and easy access to you."

Her smile wavered, but only for a moment. "Terrorists could disguise themselves as anyone, Seb. What do you want me to do, hole up in a remote cabin somewhere and avoid contact with everyone?"

"The idea has possibilities."

"Are you joking?"

"No."

"Of course not. Listen." She held up a hand. "You're giving me a headache. I've got one more concert tonight. Just let me get through that, then we can discuss this further."

A maid showed them a staff exit. They headed to Houston.

Caravan style, they went through a fast-food drive-through, making sure they had large coffees to go with the breakfast they'd eat on the road. Sunday traffic on I-45 wasn't too bad, and Seb polished off his gigantic breakfast burrito easily.

Jillie had barely gotten halfway through hers when her cell rang. She listened for a moment, then said hello several times, asking if the person on the other end could hear her.

"Just in case you can hear me," she said, "sit tight. We're on our way."

Fumbling with the phone, she looked at Seb. Panic clouded her normally bright gaze. "That was my tour manager. He said—" Her voice broke as she struggled to maintain her self-control.

Seb felt an instant of foreboding. "What's happened?"

"There's been an accident. He said something about the bus. That's all I heard."

"Which bus?" Seb glanced back at the Jeep, which was still right behind them.

"I don't know. We got cut off before he could say anything else."

"Call him back."

"I did. He didn't answer."

"I'd better tell the guys." He pulled out the phone he'd borrowed from Ryan and had a quick conversation. When he finished, he flicked the radio to a news station.

"Cell reception's really bad, but the gist of it is that they just heard on the radio about a fiery bus crash north of Livingston. The highway is shut down in both directions."

He gave her shoulder a reassuring squeeze. "Keep calling your manager. I want to know which bus took the hit."

Chapter 7

Feeling queasy, Jillie nodded and tried to process what was going on.

People had been hurt, maybe even killed, because of her. She hadn't listened, hadn't canceled her concerts quickly enough. Music and performing might be her life, but they couldn't be at the cost of other peoples' lives.

Her crew and band were like family to her. She could only hope the bus involved wasn't the one with her people inside. She had no doubt that the FBI agents in the other bus could handle themselves. They were trained to react to emergency situations. It was the unmarked, rented bus carrying her own people that most concerned her.

But why hadn't the Feds called Seb? She hoped the

call hadn't come through due to bad reception and not because they were all gravely hurt.

As Seb fiddled with the radio, the final bars of an old Conway Twitty song filled the car, and they both waited to see if there'd be any other news. After a loud commercial for a car dealership, the DJ came on with an update.

"Highway officials are telling us I-45 will remain closed indefinitely due to a multi-vehicle accident. All we know at this point is that several people have been taken to area hospitals."

Jillie groaned. "How far away are we from there?"

His large hand closed over hers. "Not too far."

Twenty minutes later they reached the first roadblock. After Seb flashed his credentials, the officer made a call and then let them enter.

Through it all, she continued to grip Seb's hand.

When they pulled up to the accident scene, three huge, lime-green fire trucks and five police cruisers, lights flashing, blocked their view.

Seb parked. The instant the vehicle stopped rolling, Jillie had her door open. She hit the ground running, grateful when Seb appeared beside her.

"Stay close to me," he warned.

She jerked her head in a nod to show she understood.

When only an ambulance with its back doors open and lights still flashing stood between them and the accident scene, Jillie froze, unable to make herself take that final step.

Seb gripped her arm. "Take a deep breath."

She did. Then another. Finally, she nodded. "I'm ready."

Keeping her arm in his firm grip, Seb steered her around the ambulance.

The bus lay on its side, windows shattered. The back emergency door swung in the hot afternoon breeze.

Though she saw these things, they registered only briefly. Jillie focused on her likeness and name, which were painted on the side of the bus.

"It's the decoy bus," she breathed. "The one the FBI agents were—"

"Over there." Seb pointed toward a small ambulance, surrounded by men in black jeans and dark T-shirts. "Those look like Feds."

Once they reached the ambulance, they learned all the injuries people on the bus incurred had been minor.

"Our people were treated at the scene," a tall man holding a clipboard told them. "But the people in the minivan were taken by air to the hospital."

"The minivan?" Seb glanced around, trying to see what the other man meant. He saw a heavy-duty, semi-trailer truck, which didn't appear damaged, but no other civilian vehicles. "Where?"

"It was crushed between the bus and that semi. Family of five. They had to cut most of them out."

Jillie cried out as if in pain. "Do you have any idea how this happened?"

"The guy driving the semi tried to ram the bus."

"Deliberately?"

"We think so." He looked over his shoulder at the semi. "Unfortunately, no one can find the truck driver to talk to him. He took off before any of us got on the scene. And yesterday that truck was reported stolen from Conroe."

"What about the other bus?" she asked. "My band?"

"They're fine."

Jillie opened her mouth, but Seb took her elbow and steered her away before she could say anything else.

"Come on." The urgency in his voice startled her. "The truck driver who caused this accident is still on the loose. He could be anywhere. We've got to get back on the road."

Numb, she let him guide her back to the vehicle, where Seb's men had parked and kept watch. Once they were on their way, she sat stiffly, her heart aching, telling herself she wouldn't cry.

As if sensing her pain, Seb drove with one hand on the steering wheel and massaged the back of her neck with the other.

The gentleness of his touch undid her. Though she hadn't wanted to, she let her tears run silently down her cheeks while she tried to keep from sobbing.

She lost that battle when Seb used his large fingers to wipe away her tears. Gulping in air, she let the rawness of her grief show, and she cried. Cried the way she did everything else—wholeheartedly. Finally, Seb steered the car to the side of the road and pulled her into his arms.

"It'll be all right," he murmured, smoothing back her hair from her overheated, damp face. "Please, Jillie. Don't cry. You're the bravest person I know."

Oddly enough, these words only made her hurt worse. She felt him shudder as she continued to cry. She struggled to get a grip on herself, hating her lack of control, but everything—Seb, the bus crash and the attempt to snatch her—all crashed down at once, crushing her beneath a weight of despair.

"Shhh." He kissed her, a light touch of his mouth

along her neck. Then he kissed her again and again, little brushes of his lips meant to comfort her.

And in a way, they did. They comforted, distracted and…to her shock, aroused her. With the tiniest move of her head, and her lips met his and she kissed him through the salt of her tears, using her tongue and her mouth to chase away her confusion and grief, hoping he would let her use him this way.

He let her. More than that. The low sound he made, almost a growl, thrilled her. His hands slipped from her hair to her shoulders, then down to her arms.

They deepened the kiss. There was no longer any him or her, just this kiss, this moment. She had the fleeting thought that if she could reach past what the terrorists had done to him, everything would finally be all right. For both of them.

Quickly, Seb broke away. "There's just been another attack—"

Timing. Of course. As usual, she'd given in to the heat of the moment, let emotion carry her away. Seb, of course, would be completely rational.

"Jillie, I don't think—"

A sharp rapping on the window interrupted them.

"Commander?" Ryan peered in at them, unsuccessfully trying to mask his shock. "Is everything okay?"

Seb assumed his usual stone-faced expression and dragged his hand across his mouth. "Yes. Jillie got a little upset. I was comforting her."

Ryan nodded. "Just checking."

"We'll be moving on now." Clearly a dismissal.

As Ryan turned to go, he looked at Jillie and nodded reassuringly. This cheered her immensely.

For the rest of the drive, Seb spoke in monosyllables and only in response to a direct question. When they finally arrived in Houston, he drove directly to the hotel, following the directions Jillie had printed out from the Internet.

He seemed to have retreated far into himself again, the man without emotions, the perfect soldier. If not for his tenderness and the intensity of his kiss, Jillie might have believed he really had no feelings.

Now she knew better. Whether he believed or not, Seb's emotions were slowly returning.

They checked in without incident and took adjoining rooms. Because road trips always exhausted Jillie, she told the men she wanted to take an hour nap before she showered and got ready for her performance.

"What about lunch?" Charlie grinned at her, though his expression was concerned. "You must be hungry. I know I'm starving."

Smiling back, Jillie placed one hand against her abdomen. "I usually won't eat just before a concert, so I'll get something after. But you guys go right ahead."

Seb refused to leave the room. He posted Ryan outside and sent Charlie and Travis down to the café to scout up lunch.

"We're getting closer," Seb explained to Jillie. "Those bastards went for the bus today. They're bound to make a move at the concert."

This was exactly what worried her. She chewed her lip and stole a glance at Seb. If something happened to him…

Jillie wasn't one to question herself. She felt what she felt and knew what she knew. From the very first moment she'd laid eyes on Sebastian Cordasic, she'd known he was the one for her.

In Vegas, he'd not only helped his brother protect her sister, but had helped Dom engineer a daring rescue of Rachel's son. In the process, he'd given Dominic back the confidence his brother had lost when he'd failed his partner and been fired from the Bureau.

The way Seb looked out for his family—and her— had warmed Jillie's heart. And the way she felt when he looked at her made heat burn low inside.

Learning that Seb couldn't experience emotion had been a shock at first. Then, as she'd come to know him, to draw him out of his shell, she'd realized if anyone could bring Sebastian Cordasic back to life, *she* could.

As she turned down the bed and climbed beneath the sheets, still fully dressed, Jillie wondered how she'd ever sleep. Overwhelmingly conscious of him silently watching her from the couch, his words haunted her.

"Do you really think they'll make a move tonight?" she asked, feeling a thrill as he let his dark gaze slowly move over her. A sudden image of them naked and tangled in the sheets nearly choked her.

She gasped at the intensity of the image.

The small sound brought Seb to her side. "Are you all right?"

She nodded. "I want to reach up and touch you, just to feel the warmth of your skin."

His gaze narrowed. "Do you always say exactly what you're thinking?"

She gave him a slow smile, full of invitation. "If the way you responded to my kiss was any indication, you'd like it as much as I would like kissing you."

A slight hitch in his breath was his only reaction. "Jillie, don't. I thought I made it quite clear that I can't be what you want."

"Maybe you did." She cocked her head. "While I normally don't go where I'm not invited, in this case I have to make an exception."

"Why?" His voice had gone all gravelly, but she noticed he hadn't moved away from her.

"I'm going to do what I have to do to help you." And in helping him, she'd help herself. She wanted him in a way she wanted no other.

Desire warred with dread or despair in his dark gaze. That was something—an emotion. With Seb, any emotion was better than the emptiness.

Tempting as it might be to see how far she could push things on a physical level, she realized with a sudden fierceness that she wanted it all. One hundred percent. She wanted Seb to need and crave her the way she did him.

Pure sexual desire was no longer enough.

Though it took every ounce of restraint she possessed, Jillie reached up and patted his cheek.

"Please wake me up if I'm not up in an hour." With a bright smile, she closed her eyes, wondering how she was ever going to get any rest.

Going back to the couch, Seb vowed not to watch Jillie sleep. Watching her turn down the bed had been torture enough—all he could think about was getting undressed and sliding beneath the cool, crisp sheets to be beside her, naked skin to naked skin. The thought had brought on a near-painful arousal, and he turned away before she saw.

Now, he felt helpless, almost as helpless as he'd felt chained to the wall in that faraway prison.

When Jillie looked at him, he saw more than lust in her eyes. Lust was all he could manage these days, and Jillie deserved more. She wanted more—more than he could give.

He sighed. No matter what he did or didn't do, she was going to end up hurt. His best option was to hope they could capture the terrorists quickly so he could get the hell out of her life.

Realistically, though, he knew he'd never be completely out of her life. Her sister had married his brother, and they were bound to run into each other at family get-togethers—births, birthdays, reunions and funerals.

This was yet another reason he needed to keep his distance. He valued the peace and unconditional love he experienced around his family, and he didn't want to do anything to screw that up.

While Jillie slept, the guys returned with soft drinks and sandwiches, which they ate in their room, leaving the connecting door open so Seb could keep an eye on Jillie.

Ryan's cell phone rang. "General Knight," he said, passing the cell to Seb. "For you."

"I really have to get another phone," he said as he answered. Their specially encrypted phones couldn't simply be replaced at a local store. "Sir?"

The general laughed. "One is on the way. We've sent it to the local FBI office. Someone will run it out to you as soon as it arrives."

"Excellent."

"Yes." Clearing his throat, General Knight got to the reason for his call. "The president has gotten more involved now. At the advice of the Feds and with my consent, he wants Jillie taken to a safe house. The man they captured revealed there is a backup plan, but they couldn't get more out of him. The president is aborting the mission."

Stunned, Seb gripped the phone and tried to think. "Aborting the—? But what about the terrorists? Surely he realizes they won't just give up."

"He does. He says since they're so clearly after you, there's no need for Jillie Everhart to be involved. He wants her protected and that's that."

"But—"

"I'm sending a team to come get her and a few more men to work with you. They should be there shortly, sometime after the concert tonight. As of their arrival, you're off her protection detail. Get together with your men and wait for the new guys. You'll need to come up with a better plan."

"A better—" Seb couldn't seem to complete a sentence without General Knight interrupting. Knowing the senior officer as he did, that meant the general was plainly nervous.

For the first time in his long and illustrious military career, Seb felt sorely tempted to ignore orders.

"That's all. And Commander Cordasic, I'd like to make certain we're clear. This *is* a direct order."

"Yes, sir." Closing the phone, Seb handed it back to Ryan. A moment passed before he realized his men were staring at him, waiting for him to relay the general's words.

When he did, they all disagreed with the orders.

"What about Jillie?" Charlie fretted. "She's in this a hundred percent. She's not going to like being told what to do."

"She's not military," Travis pointed out. "She can refuse to follow an order."

"True, but how many people disobey their own president?" Charlie asked. "How are we going to tell her?"

"*We* are not going to tell her anything," Seb put in. "I'll tell Jillie when I think the timing is right."

"And when will that be?" Ryan sounded only mildly curious, though the intensity of his gaze belied this.

"According to General Knight, the new team will be here after the show. I'll have to do it soon."

That said, Seb went to check on the woman in question and found her still asleep. When he returned to his men, the somber mood intensified his restlessness, but he wouldn't leave his post.

Jillie woke within an hour and got up, disappearing into the bathroom. A moment later, he heard the shower start.

When she finally emerged from the steamy room wrapped in a robe and her hair up under a towel, she looked like a teenager.

"I'll be ready in a little bit, guys." She flashed them all her trademark smile. "I'd like to leave a little bit earlier since this is a larger venue."

Seb nodded while his men murmured words of agreement. He wondered if they'd all pictured the same scenario as he had—Jillie naked in the shower with water running down her perfectly formed body.

His body responded powerfully to this image. Silently cursing his overactive imagination, Seb glanced at the others. They all watched Jillie stroll back to the bathroom.

He had a sudden urge to warn them off, but held his tongue. These men were professional soldiers, under his command. Jillie was their mission and they understood that.

At least he sure as hell hoped they did.

When Jillie finally reappeared dressed in jeans and a T-shirt, Seb stood.

"Are you ready?"

She nodded, her gaze riveted on his face. "Are you all right?"

He was getting tired of being asked that. "Fine." He gestured to his men. "Let's review the security plan." The Feds were covering the crowd and the concessions. He and his marines' only concern was to protect Jillie. And keep Seb from being recaptured, though no one voiced that aloud.

When they'd finished, Seb gestured at Ryan. "Let's get a move on."

At the arena, Jillie's routine of running around and greeting everyone seemed even more boisterous than the night before. Seb realized that part of that was due to the bus accident, and Jillie's relief and joy that none of her crew had been hurt.

He also knew that the other reason was due to the fact that this Houston performance would be the last concert until the terrorists were caught.

Once she finished her sound check, Jillie headed back

to her dressing room. Seb stayed close on her heels. They hadn't spoken much since her nap. She'd seemed distracted and preoccupied, which was fine with him.

Even back in the dressing room, he heard the rumble as the stadium started filling up. Houston, like all of the other dates on her tour, had been completely sold out.

Again, he watched from stage left as she strutted and sang and played guitar. Her fans drank it up. They were rowdier than usual, and he noticed that even with extra security, the guards were having a difficult time keeping them back from the stage.

As Jillie launched into the ballad that had so affected him the night before, Seb tuned out her amazing voice and concentrated on the crowd. Something was off, and though he couldn't put his finger on exactly what, he trusted the warning instinct that had never failed him in the past.

As soon as Jillie finished the ballad and began her next song, a fire flashed up in the nosebleed section. The automatic sprinklers activated instantly, and two security officers doused the flames with fire extinguishers.

Watching from the side of the stage, Seb cursed. The metal detectors were worthless against this kind of threat.

Unaware, Jillie kept on singing.

While security took care of the first fire, a second and larger fire flashed up on the center of the floor, five rows back from the stage. This time, panic erupted on the floor and on the level right above it, reaching a fevered pitch when a third fire roared to life.

Smoke billowed from three other flash points in the

second and third balconies. Seb immediately went to Jillie's side, talking into her ear.

"See if you can quiet down the crowd."

Motioning her band to silence, Jillie stopped singing. "Stay calm, everyone. Please," she said, trying to stem the rising tide of panic.

For the most part, the fans ignored her. The roar of the flames, the hiss of the sprinklers, the shouts, the screams as everyone rushed toward the exits, all blended into one cacophonous and deafening sound.

"Please, stay calm." But no matter how many times Jillie repeated herself, she couldn't make them hear her. When the fire alarms began clanging, he gently took her microphone from her and hooked it back in the stand, then led her to exit the stage.

Suddenly, a flaming Molotov cocktail came flying toward the stage. Acting instinctively, Seb launched himself at Jillie, grabbing her arm and pulling her out of harm's way as the drum stand behind where she'd been exploded.

"Come on." He tried to rush her off the stage. Unbelievably, she fought him, pushing, struggling to free herself.

Seb scooped her up and slung her over one shoulder. Though she kicked and pummeled, he held tight, carrying her away from the stage, the commotion and the crowd.

A hard yank on his hair got his attention for maybe half a second. He never even broke stride.

"Seb, stop!"

He kept on going. "We're getting out of here. This place is not safe."

"I need to check on my band. They were still on the stage. Rusty—my drummer—might have been hurt. His drum kit exploded!"

"They're fine. Ryan, Travis and Charlie got them off the stage."

He felt her relax slightly.

"I don't understand. They can't get to you or me this way. What do they hope to accomplish by frightening my fans?"

"They want to create chaos. When they do that, defenses fall apart. They're banking on having a chance to snatch you." He climbed over a fallen light cable and stepped around some shattered glass.

"Snatch me? Seb, they're after you, not me, remember?"

"Either way, it's one and the same." He spoke without thinking, but the instant he said the words, he realized how she might misconstrue them. "I mean, they know I'll try to defend you before I'll defend myself. You're my assignment, after all."

"Assignment?" Instead of offended, she sounded smug. "Keep telling yourself that, Seb. Put me down."

"Not yet."

"What if one of them shows up? How are you going to fight them if your hands are full?"

"I'll deal with that if and when it happens." They were almost to the door. "Jillie, they've just escalated the stakes. They don't care who they kill, or how many innocent people get hurt."

They made their way through the underground parking toward the cars. This time, Travis ran interference, ranging ahead and making sure no one else was nearby.

Ryan stayed ten yards behind them, while Charlie brought up the rear, gun drawn and ready, just in case any of the terrorists appeared.

Finally, he set Jillie on her feet.

"You're not even winded, are you?" Hands on hips, she glared at him.

Busy scouting the perimeter, he barely spared her a glance. "No."

She laughed, drawing his gaze. "Then I guess I'm really lucky I have you to protect me. Thanks, Seb."

Despite knowing she most likely was buttering him up with compliments and planning to move in for whatever she wanted later, he felt a warm glow at her words. A warm glow that he promptly squashed.

After all, he still had to give her the president's orders and tell her he would no longer be her escort. He could only imagine the explosion once he did.

Jillie gave an exaggerated sigh, her complexion both creamy and flushed. "Can't you even say thank-you?" she groused. Then, a second later, she shook her head. "Scratch that. All this tension is getting to me. I'm not normally so snippy or weird."

"You're not." The words slipped out, causing him to clench his jaw. "Get in the car."

He waited until she'd buckled her seat belt before backing out of the spot. "Let's get back to the hotel. We need to talk."

"We?" She leaned close, giving him a whiff of vanilla. "As in you and I, or us and all the guys?"

"You and I." He pulled into traffic, making sure there was enough space for Ryan to move in behind him.

"Talk now," she said. "While you drive."

"Give me a few minutes. We'll discuss this when we get to the hotel."

They reached the hotel in record time. No one had followed them, he was sure of that.

As he pulled into the lot and parked in the parking garage, he turned in his seat to face her, thinking he might as well get this over with.

He opened his mouth to begin, but Ryan came jogging up, tapping on the window.

Seb pressed a button and the window went down. "What?"

"Phone call." Ryan held out his cell. "It's them, asking for you. They're still using your old phone."

Seb reached for the phone. "Cordasic."

"Give yourself up," said a man with a heavy accent. "Meet us somewhere alone and let us take you. If you do this, the woman will be unharmed."

"You're crazy."

"No. Just sensible. If you make us do this the hard way, the end result will be the same—we will have you. But the woman will not live."

Just thinking of them touching one hair on Jillie's head made his blood boil.

"Drop dead," he snarled. "If you get close enough for me to get my hands on you, you'll be dead before you even touch me."

The other man let out a high-pitched chuckle. "Have you ever thought there might be a trigger? A single word implanted in your brain that can make you do whatever we want?"

Now it was Seb's turn to laugh. "You're full of crap.

If there were a trigger, you'd have already used it. Don't take me for a fool."

A moment of chilling silence was followed by another chuckle. "You cannot be sure. Your trigger does exist. We've made several attempts to activate it, but the controls we also put in place blocked it. Now those controls seem to be eroding. Be careful. We will use it when you least expect it." The line clicked as the other man hung up.

Chapter 8

Jillie suppressed a shiver as she watched Seb's face when he took the call. Though she couldn't hear the other end of the conversation, she knew one of the terrorists was making him furious.

Fury. Seb was experiencing another emotion. Whether he realized it or not, his feelings were coming back.

She was glad, but a part of her selfishly wished to be the cause of his returning emotions. Deep in her heart, though, she just wanted them all to be happy, full of hope and love. No wonder people often told her she wore a permanent set of rose-colored glasses.

But she also understood about heartbreak and pain. Though she longed for life to be full of sunshine and flowers, she knew this wasn't realistic. Her sister, Rachel, had been through hell and back, losing her one true love—Seb's brother Dominic—and marrying an abusive husband.

Then, when she was accused of killing her husband, Rachel had the guts to contact her old love to help her clear her name. Jillie had gone to Las Vegas to help her sister, just as Seb had to help his brother. That's how she'd met him.

Rachel and Dominic eventually unearthed the actual killer and realized that second chances at love were often sweeter than first ones.

Jillie selfishly wanted her own happy ending with Seb. She'd known it wouldn't be easy. Nothing worth having ever was.

She'd made her life a success through hard work and sacrifice, though she knew she was lucky to have been blessed with her voice. Several years ago she'd entered a national singing competition, which was televised, and, against all odds, had won. Soon after, she'd released a single, gone on tour with the top ten winners, and then recorded an album, which had promptly gone platinum. Awards had followed, as did her second and third albums, which she was currently on tour to promote—or had been until the scare.

Once she'd met Seb, she'd known she'd been given another amazing gift, though he didn't see her quite the same way. She knew he'd found her attractive, but emotionally he'd been a blank slate, impossible to work with.

She hadn't minded. She'd known she'd love the man he could be once he overcame his adversity and hoped by then, Seb would realize they were good together.

Seb made a sound low in his throat, almost a growl,

drawing her attention back to the present. Glancing at him, she could almost feel the rage radiating off him.

Such rage made her angry even secondhand. To her shock, she had a sudden, fierce desire to reach through the phone and grab the terrorist by the throat and shake him until his teeth rattled. Since such violence was so unlike her, she was a bit astonished at herself, but then she grinned. She'd always been a tigress when it came to protecting people she cared about.

And she definitely cared about Seb.

When Seb snapped the phone closed, his face once again went expressionless. He tossed the phone to Ryan, staring into space at nothing.

"Well?" Ryan asked, catching the phone neatly. "What'd he want?"

Slowly, focus replaced the faraway look in Seb's eyes.

"Nothing. The SOB just made a bunch of empty threats." Seb's clipped tone indicated he considered the subject closed. Jillie knew better—whatever threats the man had made, they weren't empty. Seb was hiding something. Why didn't Seb want his men to know the truth?

Jillie let her gaze touch on all of them before settling it on Seb. "This concert absolutely proved canceling my tour was the right thing to do. Now what? Where do we go from here?"

Suddenly, all of Seb's men found something else to look at. Briefly, Jillie eyed them again. "What's going on, you guys?"

Pushing the button to close the window, Seb took her hand, causing her pulse to kick into overdrive.

"Ah, Jillie, there's something else I have to tell you.

General Knight called earlier today while you were asleep."

The other men moved away from the car, still guarding it, but keeping a respectable distance. Eyeing them, Jillie realized whatever Seb was about to tell her must be very, very bad. "What did he want?"

"He's changing the plan. I've received new orders."

Waiting, Jillie felt her stomach clench as he told her that neither he nor his team were assigned to her any longer. "As soon as the new team gets here, we're done."

At first, she couldn't comprehend his words. "What do you mean? They're bringing in more men? Why?"

"Yes, to replace us. I've been reassigned, along with my guys."

"Reassigned?" Staring at his impassive, handsome face, she felt like a bad actor in a horrible play, only able to repeat a single word.

"Yep. They want us to come up with another plan to catch the terrorists. And now they want it done quickly, without endangering you—a civilian."

"A civilian?" She raised her brow, trying like hell to keep her expression as cool and collected as his. "I'm more than that. I'm part of this team, too. General Knight himself asked me to help."

"And the president has ordered General Knight to get you out of here. The president. We can't just ignore the president of the United States. Face it, you're not just a regular person, Jillie. You're famous, an international celebrity. We've seen that an attack on you is potentially an attack on thousands of people."

She thought she'd give almost anything to make his expression change. Fleetingly, she thought of the terrorist's phone call, wondering what he'd said, how he'd managed to get under Seb's armor.

Great. She was jealous of a terrorist.

With a deep, calming breath, she was able to force a pleasant smile. "So I'm well-known. There's no escaping that. And yes, people would care if I was killed. That's why I need you to protect me. There's no one else I trust more."

If she'd hoped her compliment would cause a reaction, she was disappointed.

"You're safer without me around. General Knight and the president know that. The terrorists want me," he explained patiently. "Besides, I've been ordered to get as far away from you as possible."

"I don't care." She lifted her chin, willing herself to stay calm. "I have the right to choose my own protection. I'll give the general a call right now. Heck, I'll call the president himself if I have to. I need you. No way are they taking you away from me. Not now." She let some of her fierceness show in her voice. "Especially not now."

"Jillie, don't." Taking a deep breath, Seb glanced at the other men, who were pretending to intently scrutinize the rest of the parking garage.

When he spoke again, she could tell he was making his tone as gentle as possible. "It's for your own good."

Normally easygoing, happy-go-lucky and laid-back, Jillie never had been prone to mood swings. Since meeting Seb, however, she felt like she was on a roller coaster. The flash of anger she felt at his words was completely out of character.

"Good for me? Who told you that, my mother? You

have no idea what's good for me. Or for you." She rounded on him, letting her expression show how her anger had escalated into fury.

There was no reaction from Seb—just a blank look.

She decided to go for broke. "Seb, this is right. You know it is. We can't let them take away what we could have, what we could be to each other."

"Christ." He heaved a sigh. She braced herself for his next words.

When they came, they were exactly what she'd dreaded.

"Jillie, you're a sweet girl, really you are—"

"But?" She waited to hear his version of the "it's not you, it's me" speech.

"But there's nothing between us. Not like that, anyway. We're practically family."

"Family? Family?" Crossing her arms, she barely suppressed the desire to stamp her foot in a childish fit. "How long are you going to keep lying to yourself?"

His exaggerated sigh further infuriated her. She took a deep breath, then another, knowing Seb would respond better to logic than to emotional hysterics.

"Let's put that particular discussion aside for right now," she said. "Back to the terrorists. No matter what you do, they're not going to back off from trying to capture me. Even if you go away, they'll still believe we're engaged and think they can use me to get to you."

Something flickered in his eyes, letting her know she'd hit home. Finally, something she'd said made an impact, however small.

"I tend to agree with you. But the Powers That Be feel otherwise." He scratched the back of his head.

"General Knight plans to leak it to the press that our engagement is over."

"What?" Her voice came out a squeak. "He can't do that. My fans will never forgive me if they think that's the reason I'm canceling my concerts."

"I'm sorry, but this is out of my control." Seb reached for her shoulder in what no doubt was meant as a comforting gesture, but she jerked away.

To her stunned surprise, hurt flashed across his handsome face. Emotions. Again.

"There isn't anything I can do to change things," he explained, his tone so calm and rational that she doubted he even knew what he'd just revealed. "I'm just a soldier, following orders."

"That's bull and you know it." Fishing in her purse, she dug out her cell phone. "Let me take care of this right now."

She began punching in numbers. Before she reached the last one, the window exploded. *Gunshot.*

"Get down," Seb yelled, pushing her down so hard she slammed her cheek into the dashboard and her cell phone went flying.

"Stay there until I tell you it's safe to get up."

"What about you?" Grabbing at him, she tried to pull him down with her. He shook her off, and she watched in horror as he jerked backward, a red stain spreading across his shoulder.

He felt the pain like fire, searing a path through his shoulder. When he realized he'd been shot, his pulse kicked into triple overdrive.

"Stay down," he shouted, holding Jillie while trying

to stanch the blood flow with his left hand. They'd shot him—the terrorists had friggin' shot him. Worst of all, they'd attempted to kill Jillie for no good reason.

None of this made any sense. He didn't understand why they'd try to kill her or him. What good was he to them dead? No good, no good at all, which meant they wouldn't kill him. If they did, they'd never find out the results of their experiments.

He heard the sound of return fire and popped up, peering over the shattered window.

Outside, in what could be described as a war zone, were his men. Without him. Returning fire. He spied Ryan in a classic crouch, squeezing off a round. Nearby, Charlie did the same.

Travis, however, was nowhere to be seen.

"Where's Travis?" he shouted.

Spinning around, Charlie ran toward him. "I don't know. He ran that way while I was evading fire."

"Is he down?"

"No idea, sir. Let me go check it out."

"No. I don't want to risk losing two." Cursing, Seb pushed his door open and attempted to stand. He made it after his second try. Holding on to the car with one hand, he motioned Charlie over with the other.

From the corner of his eye, he saw Jillie starting to sit up.

"Jillie, no!" Barking out the order, he wasn't surprised when she flinched. He'd used his best drill sergeant voice to gain her attention—and full cooperation. Beads of sweat broke out on his brow as he fought to stand upright.

"Stay with her," he ordered Charlie and then gave

Jillie a hard look. "Promise me you'll stay down and do what he says."

"Seb, you're bleeding." Eyes wide with alarm, she crawled over the console and reached for him, making him jerk back as he looked down at his blood-covered hand.

"It's nothing. A surface scratch." He lied. He was pretty sure the bullet was lodged somewhere inside him. Either way, it hurt like hell. "I'm fine. Jillie, tell me you'll do what Charlie says and stay down."

Eyes wide, she bit her lip and nodded. "Only if you'll promise me you'll be careful."

"Of course I will." Impatient to take action, he moved half a pace away. Her next words stopped him as if they were bullets

"Wait, Seb. I mean it. Don't let them capture you."

Dizzy, he closed his eyes for half a second, trying to regain his bearings. "I'd rather—" he began.

"Die than let that happen," she finished, her eyes clear and very, very blue. "I know. So be careful."

He gave her one jerk of his chin and moved away. Travis. He had to find Travis. The fact that he couldn't locate one of his men didn't bode well. "Where the hell is he?" he muttered. At least the shooter appeared to have stopped shooting. No doubt he was waiting to see what kind of damage he'd caused.

Ryan appeared at his side. "Last time I saw Travis, he went that way." He pointed left, around the back of the garage.

Seb took an unsteady step and allowed Ryan to take his arm. One of the benefits of a team like this was the way they worked together like clockwork.

"Ready? Move out."

"Commander?"

Seb glanced at his second in command. "What?"

"No offense, sir. But you're losing a lot of blood. Let me bandage your shoulder first."

"It's a surface scratch," Seb growled. "Barely even hurts."

"Either way, we've got to stop the bleeding."

"I've got several clean T-shirts in a bag in the back-seat," Jillie called, still crouching low. "You can use those."

Ignoring Jillie, Seb focused on Ryan. "We don't have time."

"With respect, sir, we can't afford not to."

He was right. With an impatient jerk of his head, Seb gave Ryan permission. The landscape kept moving for a moment, making Seb feel disoriented and vaguely ill.

"Hurry up," he barked. "I'm worried about Travis."

Using three of the soft T-shirts, Ryan padded the wound with one and deftly began wrapping Seb's shoulder after tying the other two together. As he did, his cell phone started to ring.

"I can't get it right now," he said. "If I do, I'll have to start all over."

"It's probably them," Seb argued. "At least check the caller ID."

"I can't."

The ringing stopped before they finished arguing.

Unperturbed, Ryan finished tying the makeshift bandage in place. Once he did, he checked his phone. "Yep, your old number."

"I knew it." Cursing, Seb glanced around him, wondering where the shooter or shooters hid.

Ryan checked his weapon. "They'll call back."

"If they do, you talk to them. I have nothing else to say." Plus, if there actually *was* some sort of trigger, not that he actually believed there was, but just in case, he didn't want to give them a chance to use it.

Ryan looked at him in surprise, but nodded. "Are you ready to move out?"

"I am," he said and took an unsteady step forward.

As he did, Ryan's phone started ringing again.

"This time, it's General Knight," he said. "Do you want—?"

"Let it go to voice mail." Seb took one more step, then another, feeling stronger, more in control. "Move out. Now."

As he did, the shooter fired another shot, shattering the car windshield.

Jillie screamed.

Turning so fast, he lost his balance, Seb tripped and fell, crumpling to a heap on the concrete floor.

"You all right?" Ryan shouted.

"Yeah. You go. I'm staying here."

"Are you sure?"

At Seb's nod, Ryan gave Charlie a signal. "We're moving out. Now."

They took off without looking back.

Jillie screamed again. "Seb?"

He tried to push himself to his feet and failed. He had to get to Jillie.

On all fours, he crawled back to the car, holding on to the open door, using the handle to heave himself up and halfway onto the seat. With his forehead beaded with sweat, he grunted, grabbed hold of the steering wheel, and finally made it fully back inside. The shooter had totaled out the windshield, and glass was strewn all over the front seat.

Crouched on the passenger side floor and covered in glass, Jillie had her hands on the back of her neck. She didn't move. Had she been shot? He didn't see any blood other than his own, but still...

"Jillie? Are you all right?"

She slowly raised her head. Her blue eyes were clear, despite the fear he saw lurking in them. "I'm fine. Just a few minor cuts from the glass. Sorry I screamed."

As she spoke, her eyes widened. "Oh, Seb. You're not fine. You look like you're about to pass out."

Setting his jaw, he closed his eyes and gathered the remnants of his rapidly disintegrating strength. "I can't pass out. Don't let me, Jillie. I've got to stay conscious to protect you."

She reached out her hand and stroked his face. "Put your gun up on the seat where I can reach it."

"What?" He could only stare dumbly at her, not sure he'd heard correctly.

There was another shot. This time, another car window shattered. More shards of glass rained down on them, making Jillie wince.

He moved too quickly, and the entire interior of the car seemed to start spinning. Swallowing hard, he struggled to maintain control.

"Seb." Jillie again. "I need you to focus. Put your gun on the seat. Please."

Blearily, he stared at her, noting how she wavered in

his view. Finally, her image solidified. That had been close. He tried to gather his thoughts, realizing she'd asked for his gun.

"Why?"

"Just in case." She gestured. "Seb, if you become unconscious, I've got to be able to defend myself."

"Do you know how to shoot a gun?"

"It's been a long time." Her brave smile wavered around the edges. "My daddy used to take me hunting when I was a kid. I know how to use a rifle. Hopefully a pistol isn't all that different."

He couldn't help but admire her courage. Even breathing brought him pain, but he slowly reached to his side holster, already unclipped, and brought out his gun.

Though Jillie's eyes widened, she reached for it.

"Wait." He showed her the safety and how to flick it off with her thumb. "I've just put in a fresh clip, so you've got plenty of ammo."

"I'd like more. Just in case."

He nodded and reached for more ammo. After a slow and laborious process, during which the edges of his vision grayed twice, he retrieved a couple more magazine clips and tossed them on the seat beside the gun. "Here. Just in case you need it."

Another shot rang out, then came several more in rapid succession. He heard shouts—his men, sounding far off, more shots and then return gunfire.

Apparently, there were multiple shooters. A stray bullet finished off what was left of the front windshield, raining down more glass on them.

This time, Jillie didn't cower on the floor with her head down. With his weapon on the seat between them, she crouched low, hands gripping the edge of the seat, ready to defend them if she had to. *She* was ready to defend *him*.

Seb would have found the idea amusingly ironic if every breath he took didn't make his chest feel as if it was on fire.

The absolute silence felt even more chilling.

"No more gunshots," Jillie whispered. "What does that mean?"

He grimaced. "Who knows? Either they're stalking each other, waiting for the perfect shot, or they're down."

"Down?" Frowning, she glared at him. "Don't even think such a thing."

"You're right. Sorry." Grunting with pain, he pushed himself up to peer out over the jagged edges of glass in the broken window. Even that small effort nearly cost him consciousness, so he concentrated on his breathing to regain his balance.

"Well? Do you see anything?"

"No." He slowly lowered himself back below window level. The small movement had caused his wound to start bleeding again. "I think they might be approaching the car."

Her eyes widened. "Seriously?"

"Yeah." Gesturing at the gun, he motioned for her to take it. "You can do it, Jillie. I know I can't. Not right now."

She nodded. "I'll try. I used to be a pretty good shot."

While she talked, he drifted off. He caught himself with his chin nodding onto his chest, like a ninety-year-old man on sleeping pills.

"How close are they?" Her urgent whisper drew his

attention once more and he tried to concentrate. Despite the Herculean effort, he couldn't seem to remain focused. He kept drifting off, closer and closer toward grayness.

Damn it.

"Let me listen." Cocking his head, he tried to concentrate. Still the eerie, bone-chilling silence.

"Well?"

"I didn't even hear footsteps. I don't know where they are or what's going on. I can't tell without hearing something."

The instant he finished speaking, Jillie made a strangled sound, low in her throat. He looked up, wincing at the pain, and followed the direction of her gaze. A man stood at the side of the car. All Seb could see was the barrel of his gun, pointed directly at him.

Chapter 9

"Don't move," Jillie ordered. Somehow, she kept both her voice and her hands from shaking as she held Seb's heavy pistol. "Drop your weapon and put your hands up."

Her voice came out surprisingly stern and authoritarian, despite the fact that her insides were quaking. She honestly didn't know if she could shoot a man.

Evidently, she either didn't sound harsh enough or the man somehow knew she couldn't shoot him. Unfazed, he kept his own weapon pointed directly at her. Then, to her complete and utter horror, he gave her an awful, malice-filled grin as he slowly brought the gun to bear on Seb's head.

"Go ahead. Shoot me," he taunted. "Do it and your friend will die."

No way was she letting him shoot Seb. She couldn't allow that to happen.

She had to take action. She had to use the gun before the bad guy did. She couldn't miss and she had to shoot to kill.

Swallowing hard, she squeezed the trigger and fired a shot.

The sound made her ears ring. The recoil surprised her, knocking her back against the passenger side door, gun pointing skyward.

Heart pounding, she pushed herself up, gun still in hand, still ready.

The man at the window had vanished. Leaning over, she peered at the ground. No man. No blood. Whether she'd managed to hit him or not, she couldn't say, though given the absence of blood, she rather doubted she had.

What the…? She listened for the sound of his footsteps running away, but heard nothing. Either way, the fact that she and Seb were still alive had proved his instructions didn't include killing them. Yet.

She had a delayed reaction and started shaking all over. Giant shudders, so hard her teeth slammed together. Worse, she wanted to weep.

"Good job." Seb's smile was weak, his gaze faraway and unfocused. "I think you took him down."

"Thanks." She continued to shake. Her hands trembled so badly she had to set the gun back down on the seat. "Seb, I—"

Before she'd even finished speaking, she realized he'd lost consciousness again. Eyes closed, he slumped toward her, straight across the console.

She had no idea if the guy with the gun would be

back, but she'd had enough. Crawling over him, Jillie got into the driver's seat. The keys were not in the ignition so she rummaged in Seb's pocket, locating them easily.

Staying hunched and keeping low, she started the car. Raising herself up just enough to see where she was going, she slammed into Reverse and pressed on the gas pedal.

Tires squealed and she slammed on the brakes. Gunfire came again, bullets striking the front of the car. Jillie shifted into Drive. "Go, go, go," she muttered, stomping hard on the accelerator.

More shots, some striking the car, others not. She had to get them out of there. Now.

She saw no signs of either the shooter or Seb's team. Knowing she had no other choice, she kept driving as fast as she dared, following the signs toward the exit. Luckily, no car came after her.

Then, from somewhere inside the parking garage, she heard the sounds of another gun battle.

There was a corner up ahead. Slowing slightly, she turned sharply, pressing the gas pedal as she made the turn. One more corner and she hit the straightaway out of the garage. Home free! No one blocked her way, no one came to confront her. In fact, she realized the entire underground parking garage felt deserted. Though this section had been blocked off for her and her entourage, she expected some security guards. They must have heard gunfire and taken off to investigate. Why else would they abandon their posts?

Idiots.

"Jillie?" Seb raised his head, his voice weak. "What's going on?"

"Nothing." She clamped her mouth shut, knowing he wouldn't like leaving without knowing the status of his men. A quick glance over at him revealed his wound had started bleeding again, the stain spreading across the front of his shirt.

Luckily, he passed out again before he could ask anything else. There was no way she was taking him back there, no matter what. He was hurt. Getting him fixed up and nursing him back to health would be something she could do to help him. If they fell off the radar, then the terrorists couldn't find either of them. If she could keep him safe and get him healthy, then maybe—just maybe—he could heal from more than his physical wounds.

She avoided the traffic jams by taking a prearranged back route that led straight to Interstate 45.

Muttering a prayer, she drove like a demon recently freed from hell was chasing her, changing lanes without signaling, taking random exits and then getting right back on the freeway. Only when she was one hundred percent certain no one had followed her, she slowed down to a normal speed and, reaching around a still-comatose Seb, dug her cell phone out of her jacket.

She punched in the number from memory and waited impatiently while the phone rang on the other end.

Finally, Ron answered. She relayed her request, speaking in short, staccato outbursts that were completely unlike her. When she finished, Ron was uncharacteristically silent.

"Ron? Are you there?"

"I'm here. I'll need time to find you a doctor in Houston in the middle of the night."

"How long?"

"Maybe half an hour."

Eyeing Seb, who looked way too pale and waxy, she clenched her teeth. "I don't know, Ron. Seb's in trouble. Please, do it quickly."

"Jillie…" She could picture him adjusting his thin-wire glasses on his beak of a nose. "Call the FBI. Or that general, General Knight. They take care of their own."

"No."

After a moment of stunned silence, Ron said, "Why not?"

She didn't plan to go into the decision she'd reached. "Long story, Ron. Just get me some help. You're my can-do man. That's why I pay you the big bucks."

He sighed. "Can't you take him to the emergency room?"

"No. I have no idea where the terrorists might be."

"You know they might be monitoring your cell to learn your location."

"Maybe so. But that's less of a risk than going into the hospital. Once it's off, they can't track me. I have to do something. I can't let him bleed to death in the front seat of this car."

Again there was silence. When he finally spoke, the gritty determination she'd always admired in him was back in his voice. "Give me ten minutes," he said. "I'll call you back."

Taking him at his word, she took the next exit off Interstate 45, heading toward some place called Dickinson. On one of the feeder roads, she spied a motel, the kind with outdoor entrances. Jillie pulled up in front, left the car parked in shadows and walked quickly toward the office.

She requested a room at the back of the building, claiming traffic noise kept her from sleeping. She paid with cash, slipping the clerk an extra twenty to prevent him from asking for a credit card. She might not know much about espionage, but she did know that credit cards were traceable. Plus, she'd wager that even Seb's people would be looking for him.

As she was parking, she eyed the distance to Room 199. Getting Seb inside would be tricky, but fortunately the parking lot area in front of their room was not well lit.

She opened the door and eyed him, still slumped against the passenger side door. As she contemplated possible methods of moving him without causing serious injury, her cell phone rang. It was Ron.

"Talk to me."

"If you can give me your location, I can have someone there shortly. He's a general practitioner who works in the emergency room at UT Southwestern. His name is Dr. Doogie."

"Dr. Doogie? Are you kidding me?"

"Absolutely not, I swear. Now where are you?"

Eyeing the receipt for her room, she wearily rattled off the address, crossing her fingers that no one else was listening in on her call.

"Got it."

"We're in Room 199," she said, not telling him they were still in the car. If the terrorists heard, they'd go to the room and give her time to beat a quick retreat.

While waiting, she began chewing her perfectly

manicured fingernails, a habit she'd kicked while still in her teens. Popular country singers didn't run around with ragged nails, but right now she didn't care.

Exactly thirteen minutes later, a Lexus convertible pulled up. Even though she only saw one person inside, Jillie sat in her dark car and watched as a tall, slender man carrying a satchel got out and walked to the door of their room.

He knocked three times and waited. When no one answered, he took his cell phone out of his pocket and opened it.

"Excuse me," Jillie called, wanting to get his attention before he dialed. "Are you Dr. Doogie?"

He looked up, squinting in the dim light. The moment he recognized her his frown cleared. "I'm sorry, they told me you were—"

"I know, in the room." Gesturing at Seb, she gave him a tired smile. "I couldn't think of a way to get him inside."

He came closer, peering around her. "What's wrong with him?"

Without revealing anything important, she told him Seb had been shot.

"An emergency room would really be best for this," he argued. "Gunshot wounds can be dangerous, especially if we have to remove the bullet. Why don't we drive to UTSW? I work there and it's not far."

"No. That's why I asked you to come here. Please help him. We don't need to draw any attention to either of us."

After a moment's hesitation, Dr. Doogie finally nodded. "I read the papers. This is your fiancé, right?"

She swallowed, then nodded. "Will you help me?"

He glanced around, as if he expected armed criminals to appear at any second. Finally, he gave her a slight smile. "I'll need your assistance to get him inside."

With the good doctor taking the brunt of Seb's weight, they somehow made it into the room. Though small and musty-smelling, the room appeared relatively clean.

They got an unconscious Seb settled on the bed. While Dr. Doogie removed what was left of his bloody shirt, Jillie paced.

"This is not the most sterile environment," the doctor said. "He'd be much better off at the hospital."

Choking back a sob, she nodded. "I know. But believe me when I say we can't."

He sighed. "The bullet is still in here and I need to take it out. I'll need your help."

She met his gaze. "Tell me what to do."

When he opened his eyes, Seb at first thought morning had arrived, but he soon realized that what he'd thought was sunlight streaming in through the curtains was actually lamplight. His shoulder felt like it was on fire.

Swiveling his head slowly around, he realized something else. The strange room seemed eerily incandescent, a trick Seb knew he could blame on the drugs. Though he hadn't talked to Jillie yet, he knew he had to be on some kind of painkillers.

Oddly, he didn't even remember going to the hospital.

"Jillie?" He spoke her name softly. When he didn't receive an answer, he attempted to sit up, but quickly gave up trying to do so. Even raising himself up on his elbows proved impossible. The best he could manage was to prop himself up slightly on the pillows, which was enough to enable him to find Jillie, who was sleeping on the other bed.

For what seemed like the longest time, he watched her sleep, amazed and awed at her beauty.

Great drugs. He'd have to find out their name.

Jillie finally opened her eyes. "How are you?" she asked softly. "It's the middle of the night."

"Is it?" He frowned. "The gunshot wound. Was there—?"

"The bullet's been removed. How do you feel?"

"I think I'm okay." Gingerly he tried to move his shoulder. The entire room moved, and none of it bothered him in the slightest.

Instead, he found it all beautiful, which was so unlike him that he had to smile.

"Painkillers?" he asked, slightly relieved when Jillie nodded. Jillie herself appeared to glow, her golden hair lustrous in the yellow lamplight, her creamy skin appearing smooth and soft as silk.

"Are they helping?"

"Yes. At least, I think so. Thank you," he told her, and meant it. "Where are my men?"

The way she looked away should have been his first hint of trouble, but the drugs had him lost in contemplating her beauty again. It took a major effort of will to focus on anything else.

"Jillie?"

When she finally returned her gaze to him, her expression was so anguished that he felt his chest constrict.

"I don't know," she whispered. "I left them there when I escaped with you."

He couldn't believe what she'd just said.

"You left my men?" Seb narrowed his eyes, pinning her with a fierce glare.

"I had no choice."

"There's always a choice." His voice sounded strangled, as though his anger was choking him. Seb dimly registered the miraculous fact that he actually felt anger, but he was too involved in the moment to wonder at it. "Guys like us have a code of honor. We don't leave our team behind."

"I'm not a guy, and I've never been in this sort of situation before." Lifting her chin, Jillie glared right back at him and crossed her arms. "I did what I thought was best. I saved your life."

Still glowering at her, he shook his head. "Give me your cell phone."

"Seb, it's four o'clock in the morning. You're too weak—"

He held out his hand, cutting her off with a single word. "Please."

Staring at him, she swallowed. "You know, you using that single word, being so polite, tells me more than you realize. You're angry. Furious. Don't you see, you can actually *feel!*"

"Maybe I can. But that's not what's important here."

"Everything's important. You're making progress. I can take you being angry with me. That's better than indifference."

"I was never indifferent."

She raised a brow. "Really? Then what would you call it?"

He thought about giving her a sarcastic response, but then decided he owed her the truth. "Unemotional. No more or less than that. But now, you're right. I'm mad. Hell, I'm furious. But more at myself than you."

"That makes no sense."

"It does to me." He held out his hand. "Can I have your phone now?"

With a small sigh, she handed it over. "Who are you going to call at this hour?"

"You want a list? Ryan and then General Knight. I need to make sure no one thinks I went AWOL on them."

His shoulder started throbbing and he winced as he struggled to position the phone well enough to dial.

"Give me that." Moving quickly, she snatched her phone back. "I'll call for you. Give me Ryan's number."

It was a testament to how badly he felt that he didn't argue. Instead, he told her the number and waited impatiently for her to give him back the phone.

"Here you go."

Listening to the phone ring, he prayed Ryan would answer. Unfortunately, he did not. When his voice mail came on, he left a terse message. "Call me. The number's on caller ID."

"Don't think the worst," Jillie said after he hung up.

A Pollyanna wasn't what he needed right now. He couldn't help lashing out at her. "The worst? That would be, what—that my team is captured or dead?"

"I understand how you feel—"

"No." He spat out the word, struggling to soften his tone. "You have no idea what I think or how I feel."

Doggedly, she continued. "You're wrong. I think I do. The bleak look in your eyes tells me what conclusions you're drawing from the fact that you got voice mail and how worried you are."

Again he felt fury swamp him. To a man unused to dealing with any emotions, the persistence of one like this—so fierce, so strong—was almost more than he could handle. "Aren't you worried?"

"Of course I am." She took her phone back.

"They better not be dead or captured," he snarled.

"Don't even think such a thing." Jillie appeared concerned rather than angry, which infuriated him further. Telling himself she meant well, he tamped down his newfound emotion and managed a nod.

"We need to call General Knight."

"Nope," she said, tucking her phone into her pocket. "I have no intention of calling General Knight. Not today, not tomorrow. Not until you get better."

Exhausted, even from this brief effort, he let that one go. Truth be told, he didn't really want to talk to the general—at least not until he'd ascertained the whereabouts of his team.

"Where are we?" he rasped. "How far from the hotel?"

"Honestly, I have no idea. I wanted to get away from there so badly that I just drove. I did watch to make sure we weren't followed."

Despite his best efforts, his eyes drifted closed. He didn't want to go back to sleep, but these were freakishly strong painkillers.

For a moment he thought the pills might win, but finally he succeeded in raising his head, forcing his eyes open and blinking groggily at her. "What hospital?"

"Hospital?" She sounded like she wasn't sure she understood.

Using his good hand, he pointed to his bandaged wound. "Hospitals always report gunshot wounds."

When she told him about Dr. Doogie, he stared in disbelief. "You can do that? Have a doctor at your beck and call no matter where you are and without alerting the authorities?"

Staring back at him, she surprised him with her grin. "Of course," she joked. "Can't you?"

He chose to respond seriously. "Only if the situation is part of a military operation and the doctor is military."

Her shrug was still lighthearted. "One of the many benefits of being famous, I guess."

Her cell phone rang while he tried to come up with a response. Jillie jumped.

"Hello?" Answering without checking caller ID, Jillie listened for a moment. "Yes, sir. Glad to hear it. Yes, he is with me. No, I won't. He's been wounded and can't talk. No, he's unconscious. When he's awake again, I'll have him call you. No." Holding the phone away from her ear, she grimaced and then hung up.

"Who was that?"

Before she could answer, the phone began to ring again.

"He's calling back." Jillie pressed a button, cutting the power off and dropping her cell back into her pocket. Then, and only then, did she look at Seb.

"General Knight," she said calmly. "He seems to forget that I don't work for him."

Seb winced. "Did he order you to bring me back?"

"Of course. He actually started yelling at me." She

sounded bemused. "I guess he's not used to having people tell him no."

Turning out the light, she crawled into her bed.

When she spoke again, she sounded like she might be crying.

"Let's get some sleep. We've got a long day ahead of us tomorrow."

He wanted to ask what she meant, but all he could think of was Jillie with tears running down her beautiful face.

"Are you all right?" he asked as delicately as he could.

"I'll be fine." But she didn't sound fine.

"Are you sure?"

"Yes. No. Maybe. The events of this day—almost losing you, losing track of your team and taking a shot at a man—have taken their toll on me, I guess."

"You shot at a man?" He couldn't even imagine it.

"Yes."

Her voice thickened and he found himself wishing he could go comfort her. "Did you—?"

"Kill him?" She sighed. "Honestly, I don't know. I don't think so—there was no body. If I hit him at all, I must have wounded him. All I know is he was about to shoot you, so I had no choice. Now go to sleep, Seb. We can talk more later."

Even with the painkillers, Seb didn't think he could sleep knowing his team was out there somewhere, possibly in danger, but he owed it to Jillie to try.

Chapter 10

This time, sunlight wasn't what woke Seb. It was the dip of his bed as Jillie climbed into it that brought him back to consciousness.

"Morning." Her smile was as brilliant as sunshine as she settled herself into the crook of his good arm. "How are you feeling?"

Still groggy, he wiggled his shoulder experimentally. Only a dull ache greeted his efforts. "Better. I think."

"Great." She held up her cell phone. "I got a text message. Ryan says he and the guys are all right. Travis was shot, but he's okay."

"What about the code?" he interrupted, his heart pounding. "Somewhere in the text of the message, there should have been a word. Did he give you the code?"

She stared at him blankly. "I'm not sure what you're talking about."

"We never text without using a pre-agreed-upon code word. Too easy for the enemy to try to pull something."

Seb held out his hand. "Mind if I take a look?"

"Not at all." She handed him the phone.

Seb took the phone, flipped it open, and scrolled to incoming messages.

The top one was the one from Ryan. He pushed to view it, holding his breath. When it came up, he saw that the first word of the message was *wolf183*.

"There." He showed Jillie. "That's the code."

"Thank goodness." She smiled. "So Ryan and the guys really are all right?" She snuggled closer, placing her head on his shoulder, curling her body into his side.

Again his pulse rate picked up. A moment passed while he gathered his thoughts. Ryan and the team. "It would appear that way. I wonder why he sent a text," he mused. "I would've thought he'd call."

"Maybe he couldn't. General Knight was pretty angry."

"True." He liked the way Jillie felt beside him. Maybe the pain medication was still affecting him, but having her so close he could smell the light floral scent of her skin felt good.

He moved his good arm, letting it settle around her shoulders, telling himself he only did so because his hand had fallen asleep.

"What now?" Tilting her head, she looked up at him, her beautiful blue eyes clear and full of concern. "I've canceled all my concerts. They shot you and wounded one of your men. And now we've disobeyed a direct order from the general."

"Kinda sucks, doesn't it?"

One corner of her mouth twitched into a smile. "Yeah. It kinda does. The terrorists are still on the loose, still looking for us—for you. What should we do now?"

Seb meant to answer, but the pain meds wrecked his concentration and all he could do was focus on her delectable lips—the soft curve of them, the inviting way her pink tongue moistened her lips.

She was so close, so beautiful and so perfect it scared him. Jillie. Lovely, sweet, wonderful Jillie. He'd been resisting her for so long and right now he couldn't remember exactly why.

He knew he was going to kiss her, but couldn't move. The hell with it. He'd been shot and made to look incompetent in front of the one woman who might matter to him, but don't think, he told himself, don't overanalyze, just act. Sometimes painkillers helped more than pain.

Just act. Just act.

So he did.

If he'd meant to be gentle, to reach up and cup her chin in his hand and then leisurely sample her ripe, strawberry lips, any such idea went out the window at the first taste, the first touch.

She made a sound. He sensed surprise, shock, relief and joy as she melted into him.

"Finally," she breathed into his mouth, but he was lost in a swirl of sensory delight and beyond answering.

The words "like a starving man" truly applied to him in this situation. All along, she had been inviting him to the feast, and now that he tried to sample one thing, he felt as if he couldn't get enough.

Felt. He was feeling again.

Stunned, he broke away. He couldn't blame all these

feelings and desires on pain medication. He wasn't imagining them—he was having them.

"Seb?" Jillie's expression reflected her alarm. "Are you all right?"

"No." He rubbed his chin. "Yes." Not bothering to hide his confused elation, he reached for her. "Let's try this again."

This time, he used every ounce of self-control he possessed and took his time as he truly sampled the nectar of her perfect mouth.

She rubbed against him, which caused her T-shirt to ride up. Pressing her bare breasts, large and round and firm, into his chest, she eased aside the sheet, slid his pants down and wrapped her legs around his leg, letting him feel the dampness of her arousal.

Lust too long suppressed roared through him with all the subtlety of a freight train. Taking her hand, he guided her under the sheet to touch him, and her smooth hand closed over the hard length of him.

Her delighted gasp made him shudder. Impulsively, instinctively, he tried to move, wanting to feel her body beneath him, to push himself into her. But he'd managed to completely forget his injured shoulder, and a sharp stab of pain brought him up short, telling him he couldn't.

"Bad idea," he muttered. "Jillie, look—"

"Shhh." Stroking him with one hand while also giving him a long, seductive kiss, she silenced his protest. "Don't you dare say a word. Not now."

Moving back, keeping her gaze locked on his, she pulled her T-shirt over her head and twisted out of her panties. His heart rate doubled as he registered her alabaster skin, lush curves and the perfectly shaved V between her legs.

Then, before he could even process how absolutely sexy and gorgeous she looked, she rose and straddled him. Smiling wickedly, she moved down, taking him inside with one smooth motion.

Damp and hot and tight. Jillie. He couldn't think, or talk or even breathe. He thought he made a guttural sound, but wasn't sure.

She moved for both of them, moving her full breasts in front of his mouth, her erect nipples begging for attention. When he closed his lips around one, she moaned, and he felt her body clench around him, the rush of warm heat flowing like honey.

As he sucked, she continued to move, her breathing as fast and rough as his. Starting slow and deep, she gradually increased the tempo until she rode him with her head thrown back.

Seb tried to hold on and enjoy the rush of perfect sensation, but when Jillie cried out and went still, he abandoned any attempt at control.

He let himself go, finding his own release seconds after hers.

Afterward, she collapsed gently on top of him, careful not to bump his shoulder, and he held her tight with his good arm. She clung to him, and her trembling matched his. Neither one of them spoke as their heartbeats slowed and their breathing returned to normal.

Jillie rolled onto her side, tucked her body into his, and they both promptly fell asleep.

Several hours later, when he woke with his arm full of warm, fragrant, *naked* woman, he realized what he'd done. Seb muttered a curse under his breath, hating the ache-filled emptiness, the awful, horrible regret.

He'd utterly, royally, completely screwed things up.

"Don't even think it," she murmured sleepily, her eyes still closed. "We're both adults, both wanted to make love. I had fun, and I'm pretty sure you did, too. Don't make it more than it was. No complications, no regrets."

Stunned, he stared. "How do you do that?"

She sat up, grinning at him. "Do what, read your mind?"

"Exactly."

Her laugh was like a summer breeze, tickling his skin. "It doesn't exactly take a rocket scientist to know what you would think, Seb." She stretched, lithe and catlike, tossing her luxuriant hair over her shoulder.

The drugs might still be affecting his mind, but he thought Jillie was the most beautiful woman he'd ever seen.

He wanted her. Burned for her, needed her. Drugs or no drugs, injured shoulder or not. "I am in so much trouble," he muttered, reaching for her again.

"We both are," she murmured against his mouth, smiling.

The next time he woke, the room was empty.

"Jillie?" Pushing himself back against his pillow, he scanned every corner of the room. There was no answer.

Moving carefully, he scooted to the side of the bed and swung one leg over, easing forward until he felt the floor beneath his foot. Then, gripping the head rail with his good hand, he followed suit with the other.

Both feet flat on the floor, he waited until a wave of dizziness passed, and then pulled himself up until he stood.

"Jillie," he called again, just in case.

A quick glance around the room told him she hadn't left her cell phone and that she'd taken her purse, which probably meant she'd left voluntarily.

Seb hobbled toward the window, the effort making him perspire. He had to find Jillie. He couldn't imagine her going off without leaving him a note, yet there wasn't one. Shit. His stomach churned as he imagined all the things that could have happened to her. The terrorists might have finally tracked them here, and if she'd stepped outside, they could have snatched her before they came for him. Just the thought of what they'd do to her terrified him.

Where had she gone?

Worse, where the hell had the calm, rational, special ops part of himself gone?

Peering outside at the parking lot, he looked for the car. When he didn't locate it, he began to breathe easier.

She must have gone to run an errand. If he'd had his phone, he could have called her—if only he knew her number.

Returning to the bed, he perched on the side and waited. A good twenty minutes passed, while he tried not to work himself up into a rage. Navigating these new emotions was proving tricky and he'd begun to question himself. He didn't want to overreact.

Finally, he heard the sound of a car pulling up in front. Refusing to rush to the window like an eager child, he stayed where he was.

As he heard the sound of a key card, he tried to relax his shoulders. The door opened and Jillie stepped inside, carrying several white, plastic bags. She froze when she saw him.

"You're up?"

Clenching his jaw, he nodded.

Tilting her head, she set the bags on the table. "You must be feeling better." Her bright smile wavered as she caught sight of his expression. "What's wrong?"

"Where did you go?"

"We needed some supplies, so I ran up the street to the superstore." Reaching into one of the bags, she pulled out a box. "I need to change my hair color, for one thing."

"Do you have any idea what I thought?" He spoke slowly, enunciating each word. "We have terrorists after us, and you left without even telling me?"

"You were asleep—" she started to say, then let her words trail off. "You're right. I'm sorry. I should have at least left you a note."

He made a sound, low and guttural, then covered his face with his hands. "I can't do this."

Immediately, she crossed the room and came to him.

"Seb," she whispered as she placed her hand against his cheek. "You're going to make it through this. You're going to be all right."

Agony would have been easier. Hell, anything would have been better than this terrible darkness, this ache. He still felt empty, and he was so damn tired of it all.

"Then let me fill you," she said, making him aware that he must have spoken the words out loud.

"Jillie, I—"

"Shhh. You're not alone, Seb. Never again. You've got me now. Let me help you."

"Short-term solutions never work out."

"Who said it has to be short-term?"

"Jillie, nothing is forever." Even to his own ears, his words came out sounding harsh, matching what was left of his soul. "I'm not a long-term kind of guy and you're definitely not a short-term woman."

A strange look crossed her face and she nodded. "Maybe not, but I think it's a little too early to be worrying about that. Let's live in the here and now, then. Neither of us knows what the future will hold. We have each other for right now. Let's make the most of it."

Put that way, her words almost made sense. Almost.

He wasn't even aware of his body's trembling until she grabbed his hand.

"Seb, what's wrong? Why are you shaking?"

The awful ache had begun again. "I don't know."

"I do," she whispered, pulling him to her. "I can help. You've let me touch your body. Now let me touch your heart."

Foolish, feminine dreams. No matter what he said, he couldn't seem to make her listen to reason.

"Jillie, I don't have a heart, just ashes in a pine box deep inside my chest."

Unbelievably, she smiled. "A phoenix rises from ashes. All you have to do is believe."

She sounded like some costumed character from a children's amusement park play. He had to stop this. He cared too much about her to let her lie to herself. "Don't do this, Jillie. You'll only get hurt in the end."

She placed her finger with her perfectly polished nail flush against his lips. "Seb, stop. Relax. Let yourself enjoy our time together. It may be all we get."

Her words seemed to hang in the air, like some fortune-teller's prophecy. Part of him, the superstitious part he'd never managed to completely erase, wondered if she knew something he didn't. But how? Feminine instinct? A hint of precognition?

Cursing himself, he shook off the eerie feeling. "Jillie, I'm never going to love you." He told himself that sometimes one had to be cruel to be kind.

Her smile wavered, but only for a second. As she studied him, he saw something flicker in her eyes, something suspiciously close to pity.

"I never figured you for a liar, Seb." Sadness tinged her voice.

He was about to protest but realized he couldn't. Looking at her, feeling as though he could drown in the blue of her eyes, he knew he couldn't hurt her. "Jillie, look—"

She held up her hand. "All right." She sighed. "We're back to square one. At least let yourself relax and enjoy what we do have. Just for a little while."

"I don't know—" But he did, and Jillie knew he did.

Still she played along. "Maybe you need some help making up your mind. Let me show you."

His insides quaked while his outer veneer began to crack, and he wondered if she had any idea what she did to him.

As her lips touched his, that was the last coherent thought he could form for a long, long time.

* * *

They'd been driving for hours in the rental car her manager had delivered, consulting a paper map rather than a GPS, and Jillie wondered why Seb never questioned where they were going. She herself wasn't entirely certain. She remembered the hunting cabin was somewhere up near Eldora, though she hadn't been there since she'd bought it from a former boyfriend who'd needed cash.

Luck, though, was on her side, and she found her way to the cabin before the sun set. Night in the mountains was dark—she remembered that. No streetlights, but, oh, how she could see the stars.

They pulled up in front of the small wooden cabin and she killed the engine.

Slowly, Seb got out of the car, walking around the perimeter of the house. When he returned, he went to the edge of the driveway, peering down the dirt road as if he wanted to see around the curves.

Above them were the mountains—cliffs and trees and wildlife. Below them, there was much of the same. No other place could be seen from her property.

"Absolutely beautiful," Jillie said, turning in a slow circle. "I should come here more often. I bought this place two years ago and haven't been back since the closing."

"You own this?" Seb frowned. "I can't picture you with this—" His voice trailed off. "I'm sorry, but you understand what I mean. Someone with your kind of money—"

"Could afford some place much fancier," she finished for him. "Like a ski chalet in Aspen or Vail, right?"

"Exactly."

"I don't ski."

His frown deepened. "Then why this?"

"Long story." She told him how she'd come to own the cabin.

As she finished, his face cleared. "I understand why you bought it, but what did you plan to do with it?"

She laughed. "Sometimes I want to get away." Turning slowly, she held her arms up to the deepening purple of the afternoon sky. "The air is better here. No paparazzi, just wildlife. I thought it would be a good place to rejuvenate, clear my head and find the poetry in life."

When she talked like that, she might as well have been speaking another language. He told her as much.

"Come on, now," she teased. "Don't tell me you don't have a poetic bone in your body."

He didn't bother to answer.

Once she unlocked the door and they went inside the cabin, the first thing he noticed was the lack of dust. "I thought you hadn't been here for the last two years."

"I haven't, but I have a cleaning lady come by here once a month. I like to keep it fairly clean in case I can get up here. Like now."

"Like now," he echoed, making his first perimeter sweep. He checked the windows to make sure they were locked, the door frames for strength and the baseboards for any telltale wires. He opened both closets, examined every cabinet and drawer and scoped out the bathroom.

Jillie watched all this with her arms crossed and a puzzled smile on her lovely face.

Finally, he checked out the small sleeping area. He noted the one bed—queen size—and the fresh flowers in a vase on the dresser. "Someone's been here recently. Who?"

"I called my cleaning lady and told her I was on the way up."

He let that one go. "I'm going to take a look outside, too."

"It's getting dark."

"Full moon. I want to check things out. Better safe than sorry."

She followed him out.

On the western side of the cabin, a shiny metal apparatus with a receptorlike prong aimed toward the sky was perched on one wall.

"What's that?" He pointed.

"Cell phones don't work too well here—the mountains block the signal. That's some sort of satellite doohickey. It's supposed to help."

Seb eyed the contraption dubiously. "Who told you that?"

"Hey, one of my former bodyguards used to be special ops. He gave it to me."

His blood ran cold. "When?" he asked in a deceptively soft and calm way. "Recently? Since we went on the run?"

Not catching on, she shrugged carelessly. "Before that. A while back."

He finished his inspection and headed back inside, with her close on his heels. Once in the kitchen, he turned and faced her, crossing his arms.

"Jillie, who knows we're here?"

Her eyes widened. "No one except the cleaning lady."

One thing he'd always been known for was thoroughness. Now, especially now, he saw no reason to change.

"I'm going to need you to make a list of how many people know about this place."

While she stared at him, he grabbed a pad of paper and a pen, sliding them across the counter to her.

Biting her lip, she eyed him as though she thought he'd gone crazy. Then, finally, she began to write.

He watched in disbelief as she filled the page and turned it to begin a second.

"Do you want title company people? Real estate agents?" Chewing on the end of the pen, she eyed him through her long eyelashes. "You did say *everyone* who knows about this place, right?"

The hint of amusement in her voice should have annoyed him. Instead, oddly enough, he found himself wanting to kiss her.

To distract himself, he eyed the door to the bedroom. "Where am I going to sleep? I noticed only one bed."

Wide-eyed, she gave him a look so innocent he knew it had to be feigned. "Who said anything about sleep?"

He was about to reply when the sound of something crashing came from outside.

"Stay here." Spinning, he looked for his weapon, not finding it. "Where's my gun?"

Jillie went to her purse and started to hand him the gun. As he reached for it, she pulled back, frowning. "Wait. You can't. Your shoulder—"

"Is fine." Impatient, he held out his hand. "Give it to me."

Moving toward the door, he froze as he heard more banging and clanging right outside the door.

"We don't have time for this," he warned.

She stared at him and passed the pistol over. "Here.

The safety's on. I reloaded it last night. But for Pete's sake, be careful."

With adrenaline pumping, he took the time to flash her a savage grin before opening the door.

Chapter 11

Shortly after Seb went outside, Jillie followed him. No way was she going to stay in the cabin without him. Not only would she be a sitting duck, but if the terrorists had somehow found them, she wanted to help Seb any way she could. And, truth be told, she didn't want to miss out on any action.

Squinting in the darkness, she caught sight of the back of his leg right as he disappeared around the corner of the cabin.

Crickets still chirped away, so whatever had made the noise hadn't scared them.

"Seb," she hissed, hurrying to catch him. "Wait."

"Jillie?" Instantly, he reappeared, his face as dark as a thundercloud. "What are you doing?"

She put her hands on her hips and cocked her head, daring him to argue. "Going with you."

He wanted to argue, but instead he motioned her over. "Stay close," he whispered. "Watch your back."

They made a complete circle of the building. Nothing appeared out of order except by the stacked firewood. Three logs had been dislodged and fallen.

"Maybe an animal made that sound," she mused. "Though I don't see—"

"Look." Seb pointed between the outer logs and the cabin. "There. Something moved."

She froze. Both of them watched intently. A second later, their patience was rewarded. A large raccoon stumbled out from under the stack, turning around in circles, panting, clearly in distress. It fell and didn't get up.

Jillie started forward, trying to get as close as she could.

"Wait." Seb tried to stop her. "It might be rabid."

"I'm not going to touch it."

"Jillie, leave it alone."

Ignoring him, she inspected the poor animal, stopping only when the raccoon raised its head and bared its teeth. The animal grunted, straining. Suddenly, Jillie realized what was going on.

"She's giving birth."

Seb didn't appear impressed. "Then leave it alone."

Shaking her head, Jillie didn't move. "She's vulnerable to predators right now. We can't leave her here unprotected."

Staring at her with disbelief written all over his handsome face, Seb shook his head. "What are you wanting to do? You can't move her."

"No." She gave him a considering look. "But we can

pile more logs up around her and make a barricade to hide her."

Though he grumbled under his breath, he did as she asked, taking care not to get too close to the laboring animal. Watching him, she loved him for his painstaking, kind-hearted efforts, even though he plainly thought what she wanted to do was a complete waste of time.

By the time he'd finished building a makeshift enclosure, the raccoon had delivered three tiny, squirming, hairless kits. Watching them struggle to nurse, Jillie found to her surprise that she had tears in her eyes.

"I wonder if she'd like some food," she fretted, wondering what on earth raccoons ate. Her voice broke and she swiped at her eyes with the back of her hand, hoping Seb wouldn't notice her foolish tears.

Of course he did.

"She'll be fine. Leave her be," he said, carefully taking her arm and helping her walk back to the cabin.

Jillie kept glancing back over her shoulder, feeling as though she ought to be doing something more.

"She's going to be all right," he soothed. "She's a wild animal. She can take care of herself. You don't want to interfere and accidentally do something to hurt the kits." He pulled her to his side, holding her next to him.

With Seb so close, Jillie wanted to wrap her arms around him and hold on tight. Each day she spent with him made her realize more fully he was the only man she'd ever love. Each moment he spent with her, he came a little farther out of his shell. She wanted to be there when he realized he was finally, completely whole again.

She could only hope he'd let her in.

"Seb, can't you see what's happening?" Lightly, she touched his arm. "Your emotions are returning. I see more of them every day."

Staring up at him, she watched him try to shut down, to stem the play of those very same emotions from crossing his face.

"Why do you do that?" she pressed. "Why are you trying to keep from becoming whole again? I thought you wanted to be normal."

With a muttered curse, he let her go and turned away, hiding his expression from her. "I do, I did. Hell, Jillie. I don't know what I think anymore."

She smiled. "Did you honestly believe this was going to be easy?"

His smile contained no hint of amusement. "Honey, nothing in life is easy or free."

Though holding Jillie next to him felt incredibly good, the instant she started probing into the state of his emotions, Seb released her. It was probably for their own good, but letting her go felt anything but. Still, he didn't want either of them to get too accustomed to the casual intimacy shared by couples because they weren't and would never be a couple.

Once inside the cabin, Seb realized Jillie was in one of her reflective moods. If he didn't do something to break up her mood, they'd end up discussing things better left unsaid.

Desperate to find a distraction, he prowled the cabin. "It's summer. Let's get out of here for a while. Want to go for a short walk in the moonlight?"

She looked up, her expression reflecting her surprise. Her gaze drifted to his shoulder. "Are you up for it?"

Using his good shoulder, he shrugged. "Won't know until I try. Come on."

Though she jumped to her feet, she headed toward the kitchen rather than the front door. "Let me grab a few things."

"No need." He didn't want to wait. "We're not going to be gone that long."

As the happiness faded from her face, he cursed his own stupidity. "Of course, I can always eat."

At that, she got busy, tossing crackers and cheese and a few other odds and ends into a knapsack.

"Ready," she said brightly, her smile fragile. On the way out the door, she grabbed her guitar case, lugging it along with her.

Outside, the mountain air contained a hint of a chill. They walked along the moonlit path, the cabin vanishing from view.

"Let me carry that." He took the instrument case from her, shouldering it easily. "Lead the way."

As she started up the trail with him close behind, he couldn't help admiring her shapely rear. When his body reacted to the direction of his thoughts, he shook his head at his own stupidity and tried to focus on the landscape surrounding them.

"There's a big rock up here we can use as a bench," she told him. "It has a great view."

The rock—more of a boulder actually—looked large enough to park a truck on. It was as tall as Seb, and the huge stone appeared to have broken in half, like a huge boiled egg split straight down the middle.

He stopped and stared. "How do you propose to get up on that thing?"

"There are cracks on the other side, like steps. It's easy, even with all this stuff."

Turning slowly, she gazed out at the trees and the mountains and hills.

"Sometimes I think I could stay here forever and become a hermit."

He couldn't help grinning at the image. "That's laughable. You'd go stir-crazy in days. I've never met someone who is more of a people person than you. Not to mention your voice. It'd be a sin not to share your gift with the rest of the world."

When she turned to look at him, her expression intense, eyes glowing in the silvery light, he realized he'd made a mistake.

"You know me so well, Seb." She sounded wistful. "But even someone like me craves solitude every once in a while."

There was something in her voice.

"Are you all right?"

"Just great." She didn't turn to look at him as she crossed to the other side of the boulder. She climbed up onto the rock, reaching down for him to hand her the guitar case, and sat.

"Are you sure?" he tried again, uncomfortable with the idea that he'd somehow ruined her cheerful mood.

She nodded. "I guess. I was just thinking about what happens after."

"After all this is over?" Seb felt his stomach sinking and realized he hadn't managed to divert her from the dreaded discussion he'd seen coming.

And he knew what she meant. Despite all his warnings, Jillie apparently hadn't listened to anything he'd said.

"Yes." Setting the big case beside her, she busied herself removing items from her sack. "Once they catch the bad guys and you're not in danger anymore."

Climbing up beside her, he sat and dragged his hand through his hair. "I always told you the truth. Once this is all finished, you'll go back to your life. You'll re-schedule your concerts and get out on the road. Our pretend engagement will be over. Nothing will have changed except you'll be a front-page story in a few tabloids. Good publicity."

At his answer, she went quiet. The silence stretched out for a long time, and when he finally looked at her, he found her staring out over the moonlit valleys and mountains. She didn't turn to meet his gaze, though he knew she had to be as aware of him as he was of her.

Without speaking, he gazed out in the same direction, looking at the majesty spread out like a gift in front of them.

When she finally looked at him, he realized she'd been silently crying. Tears still streaked crystal streams down her face.

He felt painfully inadequate, uncertain how to deal with this. "What's wrong?" Even his voice sounded awkward.

"Why does there have to be so much pain?" she asked rhetorically, giving him a watery smile. "I hear a country song in here somewhere."

Though he'd sworn not to touch her again, he put his arm around her slender shoulder. He held her as he might hold a wounded bird, marveling at how fragile she seemed. Before this moment, he'd never thought of her as delicate. Jillie always seemed so bold, so extravagant, larger than her curvy, petite frame.

When she laid her head against his shoulder, he just held her, chest tight, throat aching.

"What's really wrong, Jillie?"

A brief hitch in her breathing was her only response. He waited.

Finally, his patience was rewarded.

"You almost make me almost want to do the unthinkable. You almost make me want to give it up, if anonymity is what it would take for you to stay with me."

Desperate to stop her before she said what he feared she might, Seb shook his head. "You could never do that. Music is part of who you are—most of who you are. I would never ask for such a thing."

"That's the problem. You wouldn't ask. No, instead you'd walk away."

Despite the truth of her words, he couldn't look away, couldn't seem to stop watching her.

Giving him a resolute smile, she rubbed her eyes and started rummaging in the sack of food.

"We don't need to talk about this, not today." Stuffing a piece of cheese into her mouth, she closed her eyes and chewed slowly, making a low sound of pleasure. "That's sooo good." She held out a piece to him. "Try some."

Thoroughly confused, Seb took it. "Are you okay, then?"

"Not really." She sighed, her expression going thoughtful. "What will you do, Seb? Once they catch those guys, will you go back to active duty?"

"Probably." Relieved, he snagged another piece of cheese, pairing it with a cracker. "But I don't have to. My time's up. I can ask for an honorable discharge."

"What do you want, Seb?" she asked, quietly.

Again he had the feeling of distance, as though his newfound emotions were at war with whatever they'd done to him. Because he'd made a private vow to always be honest with her, he swallowed and told her the truth. "I'm not sure."

"Rachel told me Dominic wanted you to come work with him in his private investigation business."

Enjoying the peace, he stretched out on the rock and closed his eyes. "Yeah, he told me. But I'm not a Las Vegas kind of guy."

"What kind of guy are you?"

Though her tone sounded joking, he answered seriously. "Military, I guess. That's all I've known for a long time. I prefer to stay in the shadows, to move through life quietly and without being noticed. I don't like a lot of flash."

When she didn't respond, he realized he'd just described her life. Flash, attention and performing were the exact opposite of the anonymity and peace he craved.

She had another piece of cheese, then a couple of crackers. Dusting her hands on her jeans, she reached for her instrument case.

Feeling incredibly lazy, he watched her with one eye open, the other closed. "Why'd you bring your guitar?"

"Don't sound so surprised." Clicking up the hinges, she opened the black case. "I never go anywhere without this. When I go too long without playing or composing music, I start to get a little cranky."

He stared as she brought out the polished cherry wood instrument. "Twelve string?"

She smiled, clearly pleased. "You know your instruments. Did you ever play?"

"No. When I was a kid, I always wanted a guitar. But my dad—" Even though it had been twenty years, he could still remember the exact moment his world had changed.

When he didn't finish, she tried to finish for him. "Your dad wouldn't let you have one?"

Pulling himself out of the past, he focused on her. "No, it wasn't that. My dad died. I was the oldest. Suddenly, learning to play guitar seemed kind of frivolous."

"I'm sorry." She placed her hand on his shoulder and squeezed. "That must have been hard on you."

"It was. But Dom took it worse. He went crazy. Even though I'm only a couple of years older, I tried to make him behave. Of course, that only made him rebel worse. Mom finally had to call in our grandfather. He took over raising us."

She strummed the guitar, producing a quiet, folksy sound. "But you never asked him for a guitar?"

"No. He wasn't the guitar type." To his surprise, Seb found himself smiling.

Smiling back, Jillie bent her head over her instrument. This time, when she touched the strings, the notes were pure, almost sacred. Seb stared as she picked out a melody, something eerily familiar.

When she began to sing, he froze, chills traveling up his spine. Her pure voice rose in perfect accord with the guitar, though the words she used were unintelligible.

When she finished and the last note died away, he

bowed his head, throat tight. "Thank you," he managed. "I enjoyed that."

"Gaelic," she told him, the twinkle in her eyes chasing away any lingering remnants of grief. "Somehow, my ancestors' language goes with the mountains."

"You speak it?"

She laughed. "No. I've taught myself several songs and know vaguely what they mean, but that's the extent of my fluency in Gaelic."

As she brushed her fingers over the strings to start another song, her cell phone chirped. Frowning, she glanced at the display. "It's Ryan."

Grabbing it, Seb answered. Instead of his usual "Cordasic," he simply said, "Hello."

"Hey, Commander." Ryan sounded relieved to hear Seb rather than Jillie. "How are you doing?"

"Fine. How's Travis?"

"Healing up."

Once they dispensed with the basic civilities, Ryan got down to the reason for his call. "Intel says all communication between the terrorists has stopped. General Knight says they think this means they're planning to move soon. Word from Intel is they've reached a goal. Something big."

Seb understood clearly what Ryan didn't say. Either the terrorists had given up, which seemed highly unlikely, or they'd located him and were in the process of making their move. "Crap."

"Exactly." Ryan paused. "Are you ready?"

Glancing at Jillie, her blond hair turned silver in the moonlight, the beautiful, handcrafted guitar resting in her lap, he knew he wasn't. Part of him wanted this idyllic existence to never end.

Realizing that infuriated him.

"Bring it on," he said lightly. "Do you guys want in?"

"Of course."

"Even if you're disobeying direct orders?"

"We take our orders from you," Ryan replied.

"What's the address here?" Seb asked Jillie.

She shook her head. "No."

"We need their help." He hated having to tell her that her paradise was about to vanish, but he had no choice. They'd come for him whether he told her or not and she needed to be prepared.

"No," she repeated.

"Ryan, let me call you back."

After he closed the phone, he dropped it into his pocket. Then, as gently as he could, he told her what Ryan had said.

"They won't find us," she said, lifting her chin stubbornly. "This place isn't even on the map."

"You told me yourself how many people know about this cabin."

Biting her lip, she looked away. When she spoke again, her voice was so small and low he had to strain to hear her. "I don't want it to end."

"Me, either," he said, surprising himself. "Let me call Ryan back and give him and the guys directions. Let's head back to the cabin to get ready."

"Get ready?" Packing her guitar back in the case, she glanced at him. "How do we do that?"

"We'll just have to do the best we can, darlin'." Pasting on a nonchalant smile just for her, he held out his hand to help her down from the rock.

She seemed pensive again as they walked back to the cabin. Once there, she got out a pad of paper, took her guitar case and climbed up on the bed, murmuring that she needed to work a little while.

While she did this, Seb made the call, then did something he'd rarely done—he puttered around in the kitchen, trying to prepare something for their supper. While he was doing this, he listened to Jillie's voice starting and stopping as she tried new verses. He realized she was writing a song. Fleetingly, he wondered if the song would be about him.

From two cans of tuna, some macaroni and cheese, a can of cream of mushroom soup and a can of peas, he put together a tuna casserole thing he vaguely remembered from his childhood.

Jillie laid her guitar aside and ate what he brought her. Smiling broadly, she pronounced his creation "brilliant" and had seconds.

He thought it was pretty good himself. The only thing he would have liked to have had with it was a good bottle of white wine.

Later, after they'd eaten their supper and made one final check of the raccoon, they made love—sweet and slow, savoring each other. Jillie fell asleep in his arms, head nestled against his good shoulder, and Seb let himself drift off shortly after.

Sometime right before sunrise, he dreamed of them. The terrorists. Dreamed they were coming for him, saw the firefight, heard Jillie's pain-filled screams. He was having a nightmare for the first time since he'd escaped and trained himself to banish dreams.

He woke drenched in sweat, got up from the tangled sheets, pulled on some clothes and began to pace, keeping his footsteps light so as not to wake Jillie.

Though the four walls of the tiny cabin felt like they were closing in on him, he remained there, unwilling to leave her alone and unprotected, even if he knew he could exorcise part of his demons by roaming the night woods.

He wanted to plant himself behind a tree with an AK-47 in his hands, and mow down the terrorists the second they came into view.

Being around someone so pure, so joyous, so full of life, made him realize exactly how much he'd miss her once she was gone.

"Life sucks and then you die," he muttered under his breath, grimacing as he moved and a wave of pain nearly floored him. He'd deal with this. He had to.

At sunrise, he was still awake, though now he was sitting in a chair near the door while Jillie slept on, unaware.

"Seb?"

He froze, looking up slowly, knowing the early-morning light silhouetted him, hoping the pain didn't show in his expression.

"What are you doing?" Jillie asked, her eyes heavy with sleep.

Swallowing hard Seb returned his gaze to the window. "Watching. If anyone shows up, I'll use them for target practice."

"You're hurting," she said.

He didn't bother to deny it. "Pain meds must have worn off."

"I'll get you more." She disappeared briefly, returning to hand him a large, white pill and a glass of tepid water. "Take this."

Though tempted, he knew he couldn't. "I can't afford to lose consciousness." He waved her away. "I'll be fine. Go back to sleep."

"You won't," she argued. "Quit trying to be so tough and take this so you can stop hurting."

He tried to salute, grimacing as pain stole his breath. Giving in, he downed the pill in one quick swallow, handing her back the glass. "There. Happy?"

"You're welcome." Turning, she went back toward the bed. "Please, Seb, try and get some rest."

"Sleep tight," he told her.

He took her lack of response as a further testimonial to her understanding, making him want to curse. Why'd she have to be so perfect?

Then again, why'd he have to be so messed up?

Outside, the birds had just started singing. He needed coffee.

He stood up too fast, gasping as the pain nearly brought him to his knees. Beads of sweat broke out on his forehead and he swayed, fighting the blackness.

He felt his gun slip and was grateful the safety was on as it clattered to the floor. He struggled not to pass out, but his vision grayed. He shouldn't have taken the pain pill. Not on an empty stomach.

As he lost consciousness, he thought he heard Jillie call his name.

Then she screamed.

Chapter 12

Grabbing his gun, Seb fought to swim to the surface. He came to in time to see a shadow advancing on him. From the shape and size, a man.

Dizzy, Seb brought his gun up just as the man reached for him. No time to shoot. Seb grappled with his attacker, nearly losing consciousness again when the man grabbed his shoulder. Jillie screamed again, which brought Seb strength. He had to get to Jillie, save Jillie.

Somehow, Seb held on to his gun. Somehow, he fought the intruder off enough to bring up his weapon. Squinting through a haze of grogginess, he managed to flick the safety off and squeeze off a shot.

Just like that, the other man disappeared.

Jillie. Must. Get. To. Jillie.

They wanted him, didn't they? Where were they? Why didn't they come for him rather than her?

Seb took a step forward.

And everything went black.

When he came to again, the place had gone silent. Was it minutes later? Seconds? Or hours? He called her name. "Jillie?"

No answer. He tried once more. Still, nothing but silence. Cautiously, he moved forward, toward the bedroom.

Then someone shot at him, the bullet striking a chair to his left.

Dodging, adrenaline pumping, he skidded to a halt, taking cover behind another chair.

He prayed he wasn't too late. Obviously, they were looking for him. When they found only Jillie, what had they done?

"Jillie," he called a third time. Again, she didn't reply.

Two more shots came. Random shooting, which meant they were only trying to hold him off, not hit him.

Seb wouldn't fire blindly—not until he ascertained Jillie's location. No doubt they knew that.

Where was she? Had they hurt her or were they planning to take her captive? If so, he didn't understand their logic, since they'd said they'd kill her. But they had no need to do that now, not when he was right in front of them, ripe for the taking.

He took a deep breath, emptying his mind of everything but the task in front of him—saving Jillie.

He moved forward, trying to adjust to the darkness. Ten more feet. No more gunshots. The back of his neck prickled. Not good. He heard no movement at all, nothing but an awful silence that felt worse because of its completeness. Outside, even the birds had stopped singing, no doubt frightened by the gunshots.

He had to get to Jillie.

Suddenly, he heard an engine roaring to life, tires spinning on the gravel drive in front of the cabin.

No. He took off running, heedless of any personal danger, slamming at the front door and heading for the place where the driveway met the road.

But he was too late. He arrived just in time to see the wink of taillights as the pickup rounded the curve in the drive that would take it to the main road.

Turning, he sprinted back to the cabin.

Car keys, car keys. He had to get the car keys so he could give chase.

Back in the cabin, which was now empty save for shattered glass and upended furniture, he began to search. In the kitchen he spied Jillie's cell phone on the table and snatched it up, still looking for the keys.

After he finally located them, he sprinted for Jillie's vehicle, knowing too much time had passed for him to have a duck's chance in hell of catching them, but he refused to give up, refused to let them take her away from him.

He took the curve at a reckless speed, not caring that the car fishtailed and his rear tire sent a spray of gravel cascading down the mountain.

When he reached the main road, he had to decide whether to go left or right.

He had to make the correct choice. One way might let him catch up with them—and give him the chance to save Jillie. The other way would prove disastrous… tragic.

Muttering a prayer under his breath, he turned left, hoping he'd chosen correctly.

Jillie. Jillie. With her name running through his head like a mantra, Seb pressed the accelerator to the floor and drove like a madman.

Jillie couldn't stop shaking. Whether her violent trembling came from anger or fear, she couldn't say. She suspected it was a little of both.

They'd burst into the bedroom, moving silently, wearing masks so black they seemed faceless in the predawn dimness. Except for the occasional flash of the whites of their eyes and teeth, and the awful sound of gunfire as they shot at Seb, she might have thought she was in the grip of a waking nightmare, so unreal did this seem.

She *was* in the grip of a waking nightmare.

She managed to get out a few screams before they muffled her with an old towel. Panic fueled her adrenaline and, kicking and clawing, she fought them as they tied her up. She continued struggling even when one of them hit her across the face with his open hand. No way would she make this easy for them.

But though she got several of them with her nails and managed to land a good gut kick to another, in the end there were just too many of them.

Once they'd trussed her up like a lamb about to be roasted on a spit, they carried her out the front door and tossed her in the back of a pickup, while holding off Seb at the back door.

If they wanted Seb, why were they kidnapping her? She didn't understand their logic, their plan. Why take her? She was worth nothing to them, but Seb was everything—to all of them.

Another gunshot made her flinch. She hoped they were lousy shots and that Seb didn't get hit. The last thing he needed was another bullet wound.

More than anything she wanted him to reach her in time to save her. But once in the back of their pickup, she knew that wasn't likely. She knew Seb would realize what had happened to her once they started the engine. Maybe he'd reach her in time.

Closing her eyes, she prayed he'd reach her in time. She also prayed he wouldn't get shot.

The truck lurched forward, sending her crashing into the side so hard it hurt. Tears came to her eyes, but she refused to cry. If she could take being slugged and tied up, what were a few more bruises?

The rutted road caused her to bounce all over the place and with her hands tied, she couldn't hold on. She could only imagine what a mess of black and blue bruises she'd be once this was over—assuming she lived that long.

When they'd left the gravel driveway for pavement, her ride became smoother, and she listened for clues that might tell her where they were taking her.

Sometime later she felt the vehicle turn right and once more heard the crunch of gravel under the tires. This road also had lots of ruts and potholes, and again she kept slamming against the side of the covered pickup bed. Sore and aching, she bit back any cries, not wanting to show any weakness.

The angle of travel told her they were climbing. They were heading up, back into the mountains rather than down toward civilization. Somehow, she didn't think this was good. They were taking her someplace nearby, which meant whatever plan they'd implemented didn't include her for any length of time.

In other words, she was already dead as far as they were concerned.

As she faced the fact that they meant to kill her, the vehicle rolled to a stop and the engine was shut off. Her captors got out and talked in low voices, their language foreign with a tonal, yet somehow musical, quality.

She couldn't understand their words, which put her at a terrible disadvantage.

Despite the danger to herself, all she could see was Seb's face. All she could was imagine how he must be feeling—the guilt and self-loathing, because of course he'd blame himself.

More than anything, she didn't want him to have her death on his conscience. She had to figure out a way to save herself so she could save him. Not easy, when she was all tied up.

She tested her bonds. Her hands were still tightly bound as were her feet and legs. There wasn't much she could do except hop or roll away, and even then she wouldn't get far. There had to be another way. If she could trick them into loosening her bonds, even for a minute she might have a chance.

Tensing, she prepared herself for a fight.

Seb let out a string of curses, realizing he must have gone the wrong way because if there were any other cars on this godforsaken road in the middle of nowhere, he would have caught up with them.

The blacktop undulated ahead of him in the morning light, and swallowing the bitter pill of defeat, he swung into a graded lookout point and made a U-turn.

Driving back, he tried to come up with a plan of action, but he drew a blank.

As he was gripping the steering wheel so hard his knuckles showed white, Jillie's cell phone rang in his pocket.

He snatched it up, heart pounding, hoping against hope it would be *them,* calling with their demands or terms of surrender or whatever the hell they wanted, but caller ID revealed it was just Ryan.

"Cordasic here," he answered. As soon as Ryan identified himself, Seb cut him off, getting directly to the point. "They've been here and they've got Jillie."

"Where are you?"

"I'm on the road." He glanced out the window, looking for a mile marker. There. He noted the number. "I've been trying to find them, but there's been no sign so far."

"Take a deep breath, Commander," Ryan ordered. "She'll be fine. We'll get her."

Stunned, Seb gripped the phone. "Do I really sound that bad?"

"A little shaky, but I know you. Hostage rescue is what you do—what *we* do. They won't win. You've got to believe that."

Seb had given this same speech a hundred times to family members who were frantic with worry over the capture of their loved one. Never in his wildest dreams had he imagined he'd be on the receiving end of such a talk.

He cleared his throat. "Right. I need the full team, ASAP. What's your location?"

Ryan relayed coordinates that meant absolutely nothing to Seb in his distracted state of mind. "How far?" he finally asked impatiently.

"I'm guessing we're at least forty-five minutes away, maybe more."

They'd be too late to be of any help.

"That's too long."

"Maybe," Ryan conceded. "But we don't have a choice. And we're good—hell, we're better than good. Remember that, Seb. Sit tight and don't do anything foolish. We'll be there as fast as we can."

Not soon enough. Even though he didn't say anything to Ryan, Seb knew if he was to rescue Jillie, he had to find her quickly. They all were well aware of the limited window of opportunity in hostage situations, which meant he was completely on his own.

Promising to talk to Ryan later, he concluded the call. As he put the phone away, he realized his hands were shaking with tremors that were so bad he doubted he could even hold a gun.

He didn't need this, not now. Now, more than anything, he needed to be cool, calm, and collected. As the commander of the Shadow Unit, he should be a killing machine, ready to take on the terrorists and bring them down. Ready to save the woman he...whoa.

Shying away from that thought, he focused on what he needed to become, not the sap he appeared to be turning into. He sure as hell wished he could find his old emotionless, calculated self. This panic clogged his throat, turned his brain into a bunch of miswired short circuits and severely hampered him.

There had to be a way to reach deep inside himself and find the robotic automaton he used to be. Even if doing so messed up his recovery, he'd do it in a heartbeat if it meant he could save Jillie.

There had to be a way. Had to be.

Back at the cabin, he parked and shut the ignition off. Gripping the steering wheel, he took several deep breaths, working on calming his racing heart.

But thoughts of Jillie kept intruding. He kept seeing the way her amazing blue eyes always sparkled, her full lips curved in a teasing smile. He kept seeing Jillie's golden hair cascading over her rounded, smooth shoulders, tiny waist and full breasts. And then there was the way she glowed with vibrant energy, with life.

At the thought of the terrorists touching her, hurting her, he felt sick, near to vomiting. His tremors increased.

As he got out of the car and forced himself to walk to the cabin, he felt like an old man.

Kicking the wall, he blinked away tears. Tears! He'd come completely undone.

This had to stop. Right now.

He'd run a hundred successful missions in his day, saved countless men and women from innumerable captors, but never one who meant so much to him.

He had to find a way save her.

He would find a way to save her.

If they were going to call with their demands, they'd do it soon. As commander of his elite Special Ops unit, he'd been involved in several hostage negotiations, but this was the first time he'd ever been the one anxiously waiting.

As he was pacing, he turned an idea around in his head, then ruthlessly discarded it.

Placing the cell phone on the table in front of him, he settled in to wait, concentrating on blocking everything out but what he needed to do.

When they removed the gag, Jillie exhaled in relief, though she refused to show any emotion.

"We are calling him now using his phone." The tall one, face still covered, held up a cell phone. "You will speak with him."

At first she thought she'd misunderstood because his heavily accented English was incredibly difficult to decipher.

While she stared, he opened the phone, scrolled through the menu and punched a number.

Then he held the phone up to her ear. "Here, hurry. It will be ringing. Talk to him," he ordered.

Rearing her head back, she looked at him, dubious and hesitant. He raised his hand to her, showing her the huge fist that he'd used earlier to smash her upside her still-throbbing head.

"Talk," he ordered again.

But though she listened, she heard only silence. "I think you forgot to push Send."

Taking the phone away from her ear, he cursed in his own language. When he'd finished redoing what he needed to do, he listened, then jerked his head in a brusque nod before holding the phone up to her again.

"Now talk."

She swallowed. "Okay. What do you want me to say?"

"Anything." He leered at her, his expression making a mockery of kindness. "Anything at all. Anything you want."

Another ring. Still he didn't pick up and she knew in a moment the call would go to voice mail, which was just as well since she really didn't know what to say with her captor standing over her.

There were a thousand things she had to tell Seb before she left this earth. But she wanted to say them in person, holding his beloved face in between her hands and stealing one last kiss. Ah Seb, Seb. Their time together had been way too short.

A moment later, her voice mail picked up.

"That's my phone we're calling," she said surprised. "It went to voice mail."

"No, no, no," he muttered. "He should have answered. He has it, yes? He knows we would want to contact him."

Jillie held her tongue, still not quite believing that her life was to end like this. How quickly it had gone. Inside her were dozens of unwritten songs. The musical notes were still vague, though the words were crystal clear. She thought of the children she'd never bear and of the man she'd go to her grave loving even though she'd never know his love in return.

She half smiled, grief warring with her pride. She'd better come up with something brave and uplifting to say to Seb when the time came. Something to remember her by, not as a maudlin, sniveling woman, but a brave, heroic one.

The man glowered at her, closed the phone hard, and

opened it again, immediately hitting Redial. Sooner or later, Seb would have to answer the phone.

Wouldn't he?

Her captor began cursing. "No answer again. What is wrong with that man?"

The question was rhetorical, so she didn't bother trying to answer. Maybe Seb hadn't seen the phone. Maybe he'd been too busy pursuing them to notice it. Maybe he would come crashing through the door at any moment, her own personal knight sans the white horse.

The thought made her smile.

Unfortunately, this angered her captor, who evidently thought she was mocking him. "Be silent until I tell you to speak."

She hadn't said a word, but felt it wiser not to point that out. Instead, she bowed her head in fake acquiescence, watching through her lashes as he dialed again.

When his next two attempts met with the same fate, he scowled.

"We will try again in ten minutes." Setting the phone on the table, he glared at her once more. "Be prepared to speak to him when I return." He stalked off. She wondered if the others were close by.

She felt like she'd won a brief stay of execution. Evidently they planned to keep her alive for a while longer, using her for some nefarious purpose.

While her captor was gone, she sat in the dark room where he'd placed her, working on trying to loosen her bonds. But they'd tied her tight and too much movement cut off the blood supply in her hands.

Eventually, she stopped struggling and began to think about what she'd say when they finally reached

Seb. What could she tell him? What on earth could she say to the man she'd love all the way to her grave and beyond?

Outside her small, windowless room, she heard footsteps. Her captor was returning, even though it seemed like barely five minutes had passed.

Entering the room, he snatched up the phone from where he'd left it. "Are you ready, girl?"

Lifting her head, she hoped her expression looked perfectly blank. She nodded slowly—moving was growing increasingly painful.

"Good." He hit the redial button and held the phone up to her ear.

Seb answered before the end of the first ring. "Talk to me." He sounded terse and she realized he recognized his own number.

She moved her mouth, but couldn't form the words.

After a moment, Seb cursed. "You've got my phone," he said. "And my woman. Tell me what you want."

His phone. She'd forgotten. She swallowed hard, trying again. "Seb, it's me."

"Jillie." There was a wealth of emotion in his voice. Relief. Barely disguised joy. Hope. And something else, something more. "Are you all right?"

"I'm fine," she said while taking another quick look at her captor. "They've asked me to call you. To let you know I'm okay."

"Jillie—" he interrupted.

"No, wait. This might be the last thing I ever get to say. I'd like for you to call Rachel and let her know I love her. And my mother—" her voice broke off. Clearing her throat, she forced herself to continue in a more emotion-less tone. "Tell my mom the same thing. As for you—"

"Jillie, don't talk like that. We're going to get you out. Just hang tight. You're going to make it."

"Ten seconds," the man muttered, giving her a sly smile. "Hurry it up."

Ten seconds. All the time she was allotted for her last words, her final say.

In ten seconds, she had to find the right words to tell Seb he wasn't responsible and that in the end everything had been her own choice.

But the words wouldn't come. She was an award-winning writer of heart-wrenching country songs, but though she knew what she wanted to say, she couldn't utter the words. Besides, he wouldn't want to hear her tell him to go on, to be strong.

Instead, she gave him the words that would enable him to do so, even if only for a little while. Long enough.

"Bring them down, Seb." Savagery made her voice stern. "Kill them all, each and every one of the mother—"

Cursing, the man snatched the phone from her hands. "Tell him to come and get you."

Now it was her turn to smile. She kept the smile on her face even as he backhanded her and made her head hit the wall.

Glaring at her, her tormentor held the phone up to his ear, then cursed again. "Your woman is going to die—"

With an incredulous look, he held the phone away from him, snapping it closed. "He hung up on me. Your man hung up on me."

Tears running down her cheeks, Jillie laughed. She couldn't seem to stop. She laughed and laughed, unable to stop even when her captor hit her again, this time so hard her head snapped back and she saw stars.

Chapter 13

When the phone rang again, the man answered, shooting Jillie a sidelong glance before walking away. She assumed he did this so she couldn't hear the conversation, but something in his expression worried her. Had that been a flash of triumph she'd seen in his dark eyes?

Desperately, she again tested her bonds, as though they might magically have loosened. But this was real life, not a movie, and of course the ropes were pulled just as tight as they'd been the last time she'd checked them.

Fine. She'd come up with something else. There had to be a way. Think. Think. If she could just get out of here before Seb did anything foolish.

But try as she might, she couldn't come up with anything workable. Still, she refused to give up.

A moment later, her captor returned, grinning through

his close-cropped beard. "Good news. That was your man. He is ready to do whatever we ask. We have given him twenty minutes to find us."

Her heart sank. Though she still hadn't figured out their plan, she knew that whatever they planned to do wouldn't be good for either of them.

As the man started to walk away, she cleared her throat. "Wait."

He turned, raising a brow.

"Let him go. I'll do what you want. You can experiment on me instead."

"Why would we want to do that?"

"I'm famous—I have access to presidents and queens. I'll work for you willingly, do what you want, exactly how you want it done." As she did even when performing a song she'd sung a thousand times, she put a wealth of emotion into her voice. Sincerity. Passion. "I promise you, you'll never find a better instrument than me."

She hoped she sounded passably convincing. Never mind that she'd kill herself before she'd ever betray her country. They didn't need to know that. For now, all she had to do was win Seb's freedom.

"You are very beautiful," the man mused, circling around her and inspecting her the way a rancher might inspect a new cow. Finally he cupped her chin in his hand. "Perhaps you are right. You and your music are well-known. But you are a foolish woman." He chuckled, letting the hard look in his gaze underscore his words. "Know this. If we wish to use you, we will do so without the need to barter. You are our prisoner. We can do whatever we want."

He had her there.

"You're going to kill me, aren't you?"

"No."

"Yes, you are." Swallowing hard, she blinked back hot tears.

"Fine." He shrugged. "We will kill you eventually, yes. But not until we are done with you."

"Seb's on his way. What else do you need me for?"

But he only shook his head. "You will see. Once your man arrives, we will use you. That is all you need to know."

"Tell me this, then. Why didn't you grab Seb at the cabin when you had the chance? Why go through all this elaborate rigmarole? Why'd you bother capturing me at all?"

His smirk sent a chill through her. "Because we must utilize you in order to test him. We could not do that anywhere but here. The test must be in a controlled environment."

"Test?" she asked, sharp-voiced. "What test?"

His expression changed, as though he realized he'd said too much. "You will learn more when it is time." Turning away, he spoke over his shoulder as he headed toward the door. "When the time comes, we will use you both."

Jumping in the car, Seb called Ryan and relayed the plan. The good news was that, according to his phone's locator they hadn't taken Jillie too far away. The bad news—the new location was due west, higher in the mountains and farther away from Ryan and the team.

"I'm on a short time frame. What's your ETA?"

Ryan posed a question of his own. "How long did they give you?"

"Twenty minutes."

"Make them wait. We'll be there in—"

"No." Seb barked the single word. "There's not enough time. I'm going in alone."

Ryan cursed, but he didn't argue. How could he? He knew Seb didn't have a choice. Any of them would have done the exact same thing if they'd found themselves in this situation.

"What's your plan?" he asked.

"I'll try to stall them. When you get there, rescue Jillie. Don't worry about me. I'll get out somehow. But you've got to save Jillie."

"We will," Ryan agreed. "Give me the directions and I'll program them into my GPS. We'll get there as quickly as we can."

"Be careful." After relaying the information he'd been given, Seb hung up the phone and dropped it on the passenger seat. He gripped the steering wheel and took a deep breath before pressing the accelerator to the floor. Negotiating the curving mountain roads at high speed would require his full attention.

They'd given him twenty minutes. He wanted to get there in fifteen.

The directions were relatively simple. If he'd had his team—and more time—he would have charted out a back route, a way to bring in his men secretly while he went in the front.

Instead, he did what they wanted and expected. When he finally pulled up to the location, he stared.

The concrete structure had been built into the mountain and was more of a bunker than a house. Partially underground, it had a row of round, portholelike windows and a metal door—the perfect mountain hideaway for terrorists. Had they been operating a cell here all along? Or had they set this up recently, when Jillie had become a target? If they wanted to pick him off, he'd be a wide-open target. The caller had told him to come unarmed. Except for the knife he carried in a sheath on his calf, he'd done as requested.

As he approached, the front door opened, gliding back soundlessly on well-oiled hinges. Though he looked around to see who'd opened it, he saw no one. Remote control?

Pushing away the trepidation that sat like an iron weight in his stomach, he entered and walked to the center of the large, round room, standing on the copper X in the middle of the terrazzo floor.

A buzzer went off, nearly making him jump. He heard the sound of gears grinding and his section of the floor separated from the rest and began to move, sinking down to the floor below, which was most likely the laboratory.

Just thinking about the things they'd done to him in Kuwait made him feel queasy. That time, he'd been brought to them unconscious from a mortar blast and he hadn't been able to fight back.

They wouldn't be so lucky this time.

But first, Jillie had to be saved. Before anything else, he had to make sure they set her free.

As he slowly sank, his eyes readjusted to the dark. It wasn't completely pitch-black—there were electric torches glowing like night-lights in calculated intervals along the wall.

Finally, he stopped. Glancing up at the circle of bright light from where he'd been, he squared his shoulders and took a step forward. Once he did, the piece of floor from above began to make its way back. As it clanked into place, overhead florescent lights flashed on, all at once, blinding him and making him stumble.

He clenched his jaw. He hated feeling this helpless. Resisting the urge to glance at his watch, he kept his head up and his shoulders back.

"Show yourself," he said. His voice seemed to echo off the edges of the empty room.

The faint hum of the lights was the only other sound.

His instructions hadn't continued past standing on the mark. He'd been assured that once he surrendered, Jillie would be allowed to go free.

Of course he knew better. He needed to stall them long enough for the team to arrive.

"Where is she?" he called out, turning a slow circle around the room, arms at his sides, hands slightly extended to show them he wasn't armed. "Show her to me or the deal's off."

"You are in no place to bargain." The disembodied voice, sounding like the wizard behind the curtain, boomed around the room. "We will do what we want, when we want."

They had him there. It wasn't like he could leave or anything.

As he contemplated what to do next, something moved on the balcony above him, halfway between his floor and the tall, domed ceiling.

Jillie. Bound and hobbling painfully. Her face looked swollen, and she had a black eye and a huge bruise on her left cheek. There were cuts on her puffy lips, and blood had dried on one corner of her mouth.

Seb's vision hazed, went red. "Who did this to you?"

Tied to a metal pole, Jillie didn't answer. She swayed slightly and tried to shake her head. He realized someone had put a gag in her mouth. The dingy cloth might have once been white, though now it appeared to be covered in dried blood and sweat and who knew what else. How she must have hated having that thing shoved in her mouth.

A quick glance around showed no stairs, no elevator, no way to reach the landing a good two stories above him.

Jillie jerked her head left. A man stepped from the shadows, holding a length of red rope. As he held it up toward Jillie, the platform they stood on began to lower.

Seb couldn't believe his good fortune. What was wrong with these people? Why would they give him an opportunity to rescue Jillie? Did they really think he couldn't overcome one man holding a rope?

Seb moved forward toward the spot where the platform would eventually land.

The man moved closer to Jillie, tying the rope into a noose around her neck. He took up position behind her, looking up as though awaiting some prearranged signal before tightening it.

Six feet to go. Seb prepared himself to jump as soon as they got within reach.

When it looked as though they were four feet away, Seb tensed his leg muscles and went for it.

The man called out one word, his accent making it barely distinguishable. "Puppel."

Suddenly Seb found himself paralyzed, frozen, his entire body locked into place.

"The trigger." The man spoke again. "We put a trigger inside your head. Only we can execute the controller. You were a work in progress when you escaped, and we have not been able to test it, until now. I will strangle your woman and you will be forced to watch, unable to move or do anything to save her while she dies a slow, agonizing death." His dark eyes glowed, as though the prospect actually excited him.

"I don't believe you." Stalling for time, Seb struggled to do so much as wiggle his big toe inside his shoe, but had no success. "If you had a trigger, why didn't you use it before? You had many opportunities, starting with my escape."

"You were carried out on a stretcher," the other man pointed out. "We hadn't time to say the word, nor did we want to. We have too much invested in you to risk losing you."

"I'd like to know." Stalling for time, yet truth, as well. "Why me? And what did you do to me, besides taking away my ability to feel?"

The stranger laughed. "You are our prototype." He spat the last word, his accent giving it an ominous meaning. "That's why we had to bring you here. Your programming is incomplete. We plan to finish, then let you return to your military. One day, when our need is the greatest, we will activate you. You will then follow our orders."

The perfect soldier.

Seb could only imagine what type of horrendous acts these terrorists would order him to do.

"Why tell me now? Doesn't that make me useless to you?"

"You will not remember. Your mind will be wiped clean."

Then, with his gaze locked on Seb, the dark-haired man smiled. He leaned forward and kissed Jillie slowly on the cheek, inhaling as though savoring the scent of her.

"Say goodbye," he told Seb, moving behind her. "Tell her you love her. This is the last opportunity you will have."

"No," Seb roared. Every fiber of him—every muscle, every vein—was straining to reach Jillie. To save her. "Don't touch her."

Grinning, her captor pulled the noose tighter around her long, slender neck. Behind the gag, Jillie made gurgling sounds, her eyes wide and terrified.

Again and again, Seb fought, without success.

Then finally, as the rope tightened and Jillie struggled to breathe, something snapped inside him. With fury and desperation roaring through his blood, he moved his arm, then his leg. Free!

Somehow, by dint of sheer will and the power of his love for Jillie, he overcame whatever they'd planted inside his head. He moved and launched himself toward them, intent on one thing and one thing only—rescuing the woman he loved.

Jillie's shocked captor barely had time to react before Seb reached him and knocked him to the floor.

As they fought, the platform began to move upward. Locked in a death grip, Seb and the other man battled while the rope remained around Jillie's neck.

When she sagged against the pole, gasping for air, Seb found a huge burst of strength and shoved his opponent from the platform. As the man fell, Seb reached Jillie and loosened the rope, frantically struggling to untie her before they reached the top and more adversaries.

While the platform slowly moved into position, shouts and sounds of men fighting came from above them. Gunshots rang out as did a scream while Seb tried to free Jillie, who remained limp and unresponsive.

Just as the platform clunked into place, the last tie came loose and Jillie fell into his arms. Gently, he felt for a pulse and found a surprisingly strong one. She was still breathing, though the angry red marks around her neck were swollen.

Carefully setting her down away from the edge and the moving platform, Seb turned, ready to face the rest of his adversaries. If they were still trying to make their trigger work, he couldn't tell or feel it.

There was another shout, then a shot, and the sounds of men who were either fighting or fleeing. Seb moved quickly and came face-to-face with Ryan, grinning a savage grin. "It's over, Commander. It's finally over."

"At ease." General Knight moved stiffly toward Seb, standing at attention at the side of Jillie's hospital bed. "I hear you've already been through debriefing, so I won't bother you with questions. I can read the report."

Seb nodded and returned his gaze to Jillie, who watched them both with an amused look on her bruised and battered—but still beautiful—face.

"I came regarding your request for a permanent discharge." The general held out a manila folder. "It's been granted. I'm disappointed, of course, but you've earned it."

Still silent, Seb took the papers, placing them on the table alongside Jillie's bed. She hadn't wanted to go to the hospital until he'd pointed out that the attempt to strangle her might have damaged her vocal cords. He had no idea if this was even possible, but it sounded realistic enough and he really wanted Jillie checked out by a qualified physician.

Though she'd basically been given a clean bill of health, she'd been advised not to speak for at least three or four days. The doctor had warned her that if she ever wanted to sing again, she must rest her battered vocal cords. Plus, they wanted her to stay in the hospital overnight as a precaution.

After the general departed, Seb continued to gaze down at the woman he loved. The last wall inside him had been blown down. Through the worry and the grief, one emotion glowed with crystal clarity.

Love.

Jillie was the love of his life. No, she *was* his life, his reason to take another breath, to put one foot in front of the other, to live.

During the transport to Denver, by military helicopter no less, he'd refused to leave her side. They'd even had to debrief him while he held her hand, a concession they made without comment. When he asked her to become his wife, he wanted the occasion to be special, unique to them and the love they shared. He didn't want to propose to her in a hospital bed, surrounded by beeping monitors and businesslike nurses. He pictured flowers and music, wine and candlelight— all the romantic things that women so loved.

When he called his sister, he'd enlisted her help in the matter. Lea had been thrilled at his request and, Seb checked his watch, should arrive at Denver International Airport in half an hour. Ryan, who was now on a two-week leave, had agreed to meet her plane.

The plan was that Lea would prepare everything at Jillie's cabin for the next evening. After Jillie was released from the hospital, they'd meet his sister for lunch and then, after a nice meal and relaxing hour or two together, continue on to the cabin.

Lea was bringing the engagement ring—a family heirloom that had belonged to his grandmother Anna. As the eldest Cordasic son, the three-carat diamond ring belonged to Seb and the woman he chose to marry. Years ago, Grandfather Phillip had given it to him. At that time, Seb had no plans to ever marry and had promptly put the ring in his safe at home and forgotten about it. The local terrorist cell had been captured and with interrogation, the location of the overseas lab had been revealed. Special Ops had stormed the place and rescued several other high-profile military prisoners for various NATO countries.

A glance at Jillie showed she'd fallen asleep. Though the hour was early, the events of the last couple of days had worn him out, too, so Seb turned out the light and prepared to sleep.

That night, Seb stayed in his chair alongside Jillie's bed, his hand always touching her, unwilling to ever again let her get too far away from him.

In the morning, after the bland hospital breakfast and showers, they waited for the doctor to formally discharge her.

Waiting, Jillie seemed restless. Seb knew the doctor's order not to speak weighed heavily on her, but she obeyed, unwilling to risk damaging her voice.

Selfishly, he was glad she couldn't speak. He could read the questions in her eyes. She wanted to know what he'd do now, where he was going from here and whether he truly meant to leave her life forever.

He didn't want to answer any questions and spoil the surprise, so her inability to speak worked to his advantage.

Twice she grabbed a pen and paper and started to scribble a question. Both times she frowned and marked out whatever she'd written, abandoning the attempt.

He checked his watch. Lea's plane should have landed, and once she'd retrieved her bags, she and Ryan would be on their way to the restaurant.

"Where is that doctor?" He mused out loud. Jillie responded by pressing the call button for the nurse.

Finally, the nurse rounded up the doctor, the papers were signed and they were free to go.

On the way to the restaurant, Seb's new cell phone rang.

"Change of plans," Ryan said. "Just wanted you to be prepared."

"What do you mean?" Before Seb even finished the question, Ryan must have handed his phone off. Another voice came on the line.

"What's happening, bro?" Dominic Cordasic, Seb's younger brother, asked. "Lea called and said to meet her in Denver. Wouldn't say why. So Rachel and I are here, though Rachel's pretty worried especially since her mother is also on the way. Any idea why Jillie won't answer her phone?"

Conscious of Jillie listening, Seb told his brother an abridged version of what had happened, promising to explain in detail later.

"Okay, fine." Though Dom sounded a bit disgruntled, he didn't pursue questioning Seb. "Lea's been hinting that something big is going down this afternoon. She's got Rachel all in a tizzy, wanting to talk to Jillie. Any truth to that?"

Seb glanced at Jillie, wondering what the hell had gotten into his sister. He'd wanted to arrange a romantic proposal, not a public one. "Is she there?"

"Lea? No, she and Ryan just went to see about renting a larger car. Are you going to answer my question or not?"

"I'll talk to you later," Seb told Dom firmly and closed his phone. Turning the ringer to vibrate, he dropped it in his pocket and held out his arm to Jillie.

"Change of plans," he said, planting a soft kiss on her lips. "We were going to meet someone for lunch, but do you mind if we go on up to the cabin instead? There's something I need to talk to you about."

Eyes wide, she slowly nodded.

They walked arm and arm to the car, each lost in their own thoughts.

Jillie seriously wished she could talk. Something was wrong. Seb was acting weird—jumpy. In the entire time she'd known him, she'd never seen him act nervous, which could mean only that he was about to do what she dreaded most.

He was trying to figure out a way to let her down easily. Now that the mission was over, he had been discharged and was ready to get on with his life—without her.

Walking to the car, she held her head up and pasted a smile on her lips, trying to figure out how to take this. Her heart felt shriveled, dried up and cracked, aching inside her chest.

Part of her wanted to have it out now, and part of her wanted to walk away now, without a word, but she decided to hear his logic for making the biggest mistake he'd ever make in his life.

Jillie knew they were meant for each other, whether he wanted to admit it or not. She'd never love another. Once Seb walked away, she'd remain alone for the rest of her days.

On the way to the cabin, he turned the radio on. Right when they made the turn into her drive, one of her old songs came on, a sad ballad about loving and losing that brought tears to her eyes.

She held out her hands for the keys and Seb gave them to her. Opening the cabin door, she blinked at the transition from bright sun to near darkness and flicked on the light.

"Surprise!" Several voices hollered.

Jillie jumped back into Seb, who appeared as stunned as she.

Lea rushed forward, hugging her. Then came Rachel and Dominic. Finally, Seb's mother, smiling serenely, enveloped Jillie in a vanilla-scented hug.

Jillie turned to look at Seb, questioning him with her

eyes. At first, he looked angry. Then, meeting Jillie's gaze, he shook his head, gave her a resigned smile and held out his hand to his sister.

Grinning broadly, Lea dropped something into his hand and stepped back, linking arms with the rest of the family.

Seb regained her attention by tugging on her hand. Then, to her disbelief, he dropped to one knee in front of her, gazing up at her with love in his face.

"Jillie, I—" He choked up before he could finish speaking. As she stared in shock, the former Special Ops commander and emotionless man broke down, covering his eyes with his hands.

Concerned, Jillie dropped to the floor with him, wrapping her arms around him and kissing his face while his family looked on.

He wiped at his eyes with the back of his hand, smiling at her through his tears. "I'm sorry," he murmured and then kissed her deeply. He tasted of salt, which made her smile.

Then, taking her left hand, he opened his closed fist and showed her a ring. The huge diamond sparkled in an antique setting.

As she stared, he kissed her again and slipped the ring on her finger. "Will you do me the honor of becoming my wife?"

Though she couldn't say the words out loud, she gave him her answer by wrapping her arms around his neck and giving him a long, deep kiss, full of love.

One by one, his family began cheering.

"Welcome to the family," Dom and Lea said in unison.

Rachel stepped forward, enveloping them both in a hug. "Must be a family tradition," she whispered in Jillie's ear, reminding her that Dominic had also proposed with the Cordasic family gathered round.

"It is," Seb said, rising and pulling Jillie up after him. "I'd like to present the future Mrs. Sebastian Cor—"

Jillie interrupted him with a touch, motioning to Rachel to explain. She'd talked to her sister about this many times.

"She'll have to keep her name because of the recording career," Rachel began. Waving her hand, Jillie interrupted again, wishing she could speak, only a little.

She grabbed a pad and pen and wrote down what she wanted Seb to know. When she handed this to him, he began to laugh.

"Cordasic-Everhart," he said. "Hyphenated."

"Of course." Rachel sounded relieved.

Jillie only had eyes for Seb, wondering how he'd take this. She knew how proud he was of his illustrious family name.

"Of course," he murmured also, then sealed the deal with a passionate kiss, making Jillie wish she could get him alone.

Seb's answering grin contained a promise. "Soon," he whispered. "Soon."

Then, arm and arm, they turned to face the family. Together. Now and for always.

* * * * *

Celebrate 60 years of pure reading pleasure with Harlequin®!

Step back in time and enjoy a sneak preview of an exciting anthology from Harlequin® Historical with
THE DIAMONDS OF WELBOURNE MANOR

This compelling anthology features three stories about the outrageous Fitzmanning sisters. Meet Annalise, who is never at a loss for words… But that can change with an unexpected encounter in the forest.

Available May 2009 from Harlequin® Historical.

"I'm the illegitimate daughter of notoriously scandalous parents, Mr. Milford. Candidates for my hand are unlikely to be lining up at the gates."

"Don't be so quick to discount your charms, my dear. Or the charm of your substantial dowry. Or even your brothers' influence. There are as many reasons to marry as there are marriages."

Annalise snorted. "Oh, yes. Perhaps I shall marry for dynastic reasons, or perhaps for property or influence. After all, a loveless, practical marriage worked out so well for my mother."

"Well, you've routed me on that one. I can think of no suitable rejoinder." Ned rose to his feet and extended his hand. "And since that is the case, let me be the first to wish you a long and happy spinsterhood."

Her mouth gaped open. And then she laughed.

And he froze.

This was the first time, Ned realized. The first time he'd seen her eyes light up and her mouth curl. The first time he'd witnessed her features melded together in glorious accord to produce exquisite beauty.

Unbelievable what a change came over her face. Unheard of what effect her throaty, rasping laughter had on his body. It pounded a beat upon his ear, quickly taken up by his pulse. It echoed through him, finally residing in his stirring nether regions.

So easily she did it, awakened these sensations within him—without any apparent effort at all. And she had called him potentially dangerous? Clearly the intelligent thing for him to do would be to steer clear, to leave her to the tender ministrations of Lord Peter Blackthorne.

"You were right." She smiled up at him as she took his hand and climbed to her feet. "I do feel better."

Ah, well. When had he ever chosen the intelligent path?

He did not relinquish her hand. He used it to pull her in, close enough that he could feel the warmth of her. "At the risk of repeating Lord Peter's mistake and anticipating too much—may I ask if you'll be my partner in battledore tomorrow?"

Her smiled dimmed. Her breath came a little faster. His own had gone shallow, as if he'd just run a race—and lost. He ran his gaze over the appealing lift of her brow and the curious angle of her chin. His index finger twitched.

"I should like that," she said.

His finger trembled again and he lifted it, traced the

pink and tender shell of her ear, the unique sweep of her jaw. Her pulse leaped beneath her skin, triggering his own. Slowly he tilted her chin up, waiting for her to object, to step back, to slap his hand away.

She did none of those eminently sensible things. Which left him free to do the entirely impractical thing.

Baby soft, the skin of her lips. Her whole body trembled when he touched her there.

He leaned in. Her eyes closed, even as she stood straight against him, strung as tight as a bow. He pressed his mouth to hers. It was a soft kiss, sweet and chaste. And yet he was hot and hard and as ready as he'd ever been in his life.

She drew back a little. Sighed. Their breath mingled a moment before she slowly backed away.

"Oh," she breathed. Her dark eyes were full of wonder and something that looked like fear. He took a step toward her, but she only shook her head. His outstretched hand fell to his side as she turned to disappear into the wood. This was the first time, Ned realized. The first time, since he'd come to the house party at Welbourne Manor, that he'd seen her eyes light up.

* * * * *

Follow Ned and Annalise's story in May 2009 in
THE DIAMONDS OF WELBOURNE MANOR
Available May 2009 from Harlequin® Historical

Available in the series romance section, or in the historical romance section, wherever books are sold.

**We'll be spotlighting a different series
every month throughout 2009
to celebrate our 60th anniversary.**

Look for Harlequin® Historical in May!

Celebrations begin with
a sumptuous Regency house party!

Join three scandalous sisters in

**THE DIAMONDS OF
WELBOURNE MANOR**

Glittering, scintillating, sensual fun
by Diane Gaston, Deb Marlowe
and Amanda McCabe.

**60 years of Harlequin,
600 years of romance
in Harlequin Historical!**

REQUEST YOUR FREE BOOKS!

2 FREE NOVELS PLUS 2 FREE GIFTS!

Silhouette® Romantic SUSPENSE

Sparked by Danger, Fueled by Passion!

YES! Please send me 2 FREE Silhouette® Romantic Suspense novels and my 2 FREE gifts (gifts are worth about $10). After receiving them, if I don't wish to receive any more books, I can return the shipping statement marked "cancel." If I don't cancel, I will receive 4 brand-new novels every month and be billed just $4.24 per book in the U.S. or $4.99 per book in Canada. That's a savings of at least 15% off the cover price! It's quite a bargain! Shipping and handling is just 25¢ per book*. I understand that accepting the 2 free books and gifts places me under no obligation to buy anything. I can always return a shipment and cancel at any time. Even if I never buy another book from Silhouette, the two free books and gifts are mine to keep forever.

240 SDN EEX6   340 SDN EEYJ

Name	(PLEASE PRINT)

Address	Apt. #

City	State/Prov.	Zip/Postal Code

Signature (if under 18, a parent or guardian must sign)

Mail to the Silhouette Reader Service:
IN U.S.A.: P.O. Box 1867, Buffalo, NY 14240-1867
IN CANADA: P.O. Box 609, Fort Erie, Ontario L2A 5X3

Not valid to current subscribers of Silhouette Romantic Suspense books.

Want to try two free books from another line?
Call 1-800-873-8635 or visit www.morefreebooks.com.

* Terms and prices subject to change without notice. Prices do not include applicable taxes. Sales tax applicable in N.Y. Canadian residents will be charged applicable provincial taxes and GST. Offer not valid in Quebec. This offer is limited to one order per household. All orders subject to approval. Credit or debit balances in a customer's account(s) may be offset by any other outstanding balance owed by or to the customer. Please allow 4 to 6 weeks for delivery. Offer available while quantities last.

Your Privacy: Silhouette is committed to protecting your privacy. Our Privacy Policy is available online at www.eHarlequin.com or upon request from the Reader Service. From time to time we make our lists of customers available to reputable third parties who may have a product or service of interest to you. If you would prefer we not share your name and address, please check here. ☐

SR®

You're invited to join our Tell Harlequin Reader Panel!

By joining our new reader panel you will:

- Receive Harlequin® books—they are FREE and yours to keep with no obligation to purchase anything!
- Participate in fun online surveys
- Exchange opinions and ideas with women just like you
- Have a say in our new book ideas and help us publish the best in women's fiction

In addition, you will have a chance to win great prizes and receive special gifts!
See Web site for details. Some conditions apply.
Space is limited.

To join, visit us at
www.TellHarlequin.com.

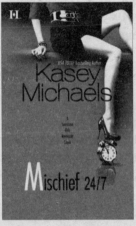

Harlequin® Historical
Historical Romantic Adventure!

If you enjoyed reading
Joanne Rock in the
Harlequin® Blaze™ series,
look for her new book
from Harlequin® Historical!

THE KNIGHT'S RETURN
Joanne Rock

Missing more than his memory,
Hugh de Montagne sets out to find his
true identity. When he lands in a small
Irish kingdom and finds a new liege in the
Irish king, his hands are full with his new
assignment: guarding the king's beautiful,
exiled daughter. Sorcha has had her heart
broken by a knight in the past. Will she be
able to open her heart to love again?

Available April
wherever books are sold.

Romantic
SUSPENSE

COMING NEXT MONTH

Available April 28, 2009

#1559 LADY KILLER—Kathleen Creighton
The Taken
When Tony Whitehall is enlisted to find out more about
Brooke Fallon Grant, who's accused of murdering her abusive ex-husband,
she insists that she—and her pet cougar, Lady—are
innocent. Sparks fly between Tony and Brooke as they try to save
the animal's life and discover who the killer really is.

#1560 HIS 7-DAY FIANCÉE—Gail Barrett
Love in 60 Seconds
Starting a new life in Las Vegas, Amanda Patterson never predicted she'd
be assaulted by a gunman in a casino. Owner Luke Montgomery fears bad
publicity and convinces her to keep quiet. When someone tries to kidnap
her daughter, Amanda agrees to Luke's plan to temporarily move in with
him and act as his fiancée, but their growing attraction soon puts them all
in danger.

#1561 NIGHT RESCUER—Cindy Dees
H.O.T. Watch
Wracked with survivor's guilt, former Special Forces agent
John Hollister agrees to put his suicide on hold to deliver medical
researcher Melina Montez to the mountains of Peru. As sexual heat and
desire flare, she reveals the fatal mission she's on to rescue her family,
and together they challenge each other to fight to stay alive for love.

#1562 HIGH-STAKES HOMECOMING—Suzanne McMinn
Haven
Intending to lay claim to his inherited family farm, Penn Ramsey is
shocked to discover the woman who once broke his heart. Willa also
claims the farm is hers, and when a storm strands them at the house
together, they discover their attraction hasn't died and all isn't as it seems.
Is the house trying to keep them from leaving? Or is something—or
someone—else at work here?

SRSCNMBPA0409